A Candlelight Ecstasy Romance

"A THOUSAND TIMES I'VE WISHED I COULD GO BACK AND CHANGE IT ALL," KALER BURST OUT.

"I know that!" cried Beth. She'd hurt him and in hurting him she'd pained herself unbearably. "I'm sorry. I didn't mean to stir up old wounds. What happened then doesn't matter."

"It does matter. It matters every time I see someone avoid me, every time I realize how much of my life I wasted. But if I can't change the past, I can change the man. And believe me, I've changed."

"I know you have," she said. "What you did never seemed to match up with the man I know you are. I wanted to understand it. Thank you for explaining."

Joyous relief flooded his soul, lightening and lifting him. She didn't hate him; she didn't even think less of him. "You don't need to thank me. I wanted to explain. I wanted you to know that I'm trying to turn things around. It's so easy to go wrong and so damned difficult to set it all right again."

"How many men even try?" she asked in a soft whisper.

CANDLELIGHT ECSTASY ROMANCES®

SINNER AND SAINT

Prudence Martin

A CANDLELIGHT ECSTASY ROMANCE®

Published by
Dell Publishing Co., Inc.
1 Dag Hammarskjold Plaza
New York, New York 10017

Dell ® TM 681510, Dell Publishing Co., Inc.

Candlelight Ecstasy Romance®, 1,203,540, is a registered
trademark of Dell Publishing Co., Inc.,
New York, New York.

ISBN: 0-440-18140-2

Printed in the United States of America
First printing—October 1984

to John
for helping me
to understand

To Our Readers:

We have been delighted with your enthusiastic response to Candlelight Ecstasy Romances®, and we thank you for the interest you have shown in this exciting series.

In the upcoming months we will continue to present the distinctive sensuous love stories you have come to expect only from Ecstasy. We look forward to bringing you many more books from your favorite authors and also, the very finest work from new authors of contemporary romantic fiction.

As always, we are striving to present the unique, absorbing love stories that you enjoy most—books that are more than ordinary romance.
Your suggestions and comments are always welcome. Please write to us at the address below.

Sincerely,

The Editors
Candlelight Romances
1 Dag Hammarskjold Plaza
New York, New York 10017

CHAPTER ONE

Martha Hanson stated emphatically that she, for one, would start locking her doors at night.

A rare murmur of accord rippled through the circle of women crowded into the Rasmussens' old-fashioned living room. Beth stared at them all in amused astonishment. Accord was not common among the ladies of her home extension group, far from it. Whether discussing the annual fund-raiser charity bazaar, the county elections, or even a subject as mundane as the weather, the women could usually be counted on for an hour or two of heated debate. Such disputes almost always carried over for a few meetings, adding fuel to the next disagreement, and the next. Apparently not this time. Even Harriet Trowbridge echoed Martha's pronouncement without so much as a pause for breath, although just last week Harriet had insisted Martha Hanson didn't have enough brains to fill a thimble. A mischievous impulse, or perhaps the streak of contrariness her mother had so often complained about, compelled Beth to dissent.

"That's a shade dramatic, don't you think?" she asked, and knew the satisfaction of instantaneous results.

Ten heads swiveled, ten pairs of eyes focused sharply on her. The grandfather clock in the corner ticked loudly, the wind sang with the rustling of leaves from beyond the screened windows. A muffled undertone of voices drifted

11

in from the den, where the rest of the family was watching television. Beth heard each sound distinctly in the same instant that a coffee cup clattered to its saucer and the group's attention shifted to the high-backed chair where Martha sat, her wiry figure erect, her smile a stiff line on her wrinkled face.

"Dramatic? What do you mean, dramatic?"

Beth took the time to lower her own cup to its saucer and smile at them all before replying. "It just seems to me that you're blowing things out of proportion, locking your doors. After all, it's not as if he's a rapist or anything."

Like a string abruptly yanked, the line of Martha's mouth puckered into sharp ridges of disapproval. "Really, my dear," she huffed, "we all know *precisely* what he is."

"Then you should know what he isn't. He isn't the boogeyman."

Beth's vehemence surprised even herself. Her earlier amusement had completely subsided, deflated by a prick of annoyance. What was the matter with all of them? Weren't they going to give the poor man a chance?

Shocked glances passed from one woman to another, sweeping the circle in a matter of seconds. No one, however, dared to meet the reproach in Beth's clear blue gaze.

"Still, it never hurts to take precautions," Sally Green said at last. The young brunette glanced down at her bulging stomach, her plump, rosy cheeks growing rosier as she folded her hands protectively across her ballooning belly. "You'll realize that once you start having a family, Beth."

"She'd better get married first," put in Candace Rasmussen dryly and Beth rolled her eyes at her sister-in-law while the others laughed.

Beth knew she should let the matter drop and end the

evening on a note of camaraderie. But the bur was under her skin and wouldn't let her be. As the laughter resounded, her irritation with them grew unreasonably until she heard herself stoutly saying, "Even if I had ten kids, it wouldn't change my opinion. I think you're all overreacting. He's home barely one day and you're ready to run him out of town on a rail."

"What would you have us do?" demanded Patsy Lackey. She threw out her long arms. "Welcome him back with a party?"

"No, but—"

"That wild O'Connell boy will probably give his own party," Martha asserted with a decided sniff that said just what kind of a party it would be.

Tongues clicked in agreement. Beth had to bite hers to keep from shouting at them. She wondered why she felt so strongly. What, after all, did it matter to her? She didn't care anything about O'Connell; she'd hardly known him at all, and that mostly by reputation. Yet she continued to defend him.

"He's hardly a boy any longer," she pointed out as calmly as she could.

"No, he's not," Martha agreed on a bite. "Now he's a—"

"And he didn't look at all wild to me. Far from it."

Once again all eyes riveted on Beth. She gripped her hands in her lap and wished she'd kept her mouth shut. Would she never learn? She squirmed and the hardwood rocker swayed slightly. "I only meant that I saw him walking away from the bus station this afternoon and he looked no different from anyone else, just a regular person, that's all."

But he hadn't, her mind shrieked in protest. He hadn't looked like a regular person at all. From the moment he'd stepped out onto the street, he'd stood out from everyone else. Perhaps it was because other people stopped and

13

stared, giving him wide berth on the sidewalk. Or perhaps it was his outdated brown suit or the battered condition of his suitcase, but Beth didn't really think so. Beth thought it was because Kaler O'Connell was the type of man who would always stand out in a crowd, the type of man no one could forget.

And it was obvious they hadn't forgotten.

"That O'Connell never looked like anybody else," Ruth Doyle exclaimed, sounding shocked at the suggestion.

"Didn't act like anybody else either. Seemed to think he could live by his own rules."

"He was always a real loner, that O'Connell boy."

"He had a way of looking right through a body that turned my blood to ice."

"He had a chip on his shoulder. Too much pride, that was his problem."

"*One* of his problems!"

"Well, now, he was always very polite as a boy, always minded his manners at the shop," murmured Irene Bauer in her whispery voice. "He never took a bit of candy from me without saying thank you. There was good in him back then. Perhaps there still is."

"Oh, Irene, you'd think good of the devil himself, you would," Ruth added.

"But maybe she's right. You could at least give him the benefit of the doubt."

"You're too trusting, Beth. When you get a little older you'll realize. People can be very disillusioning." Harriet stared for a time at her coffee. She brushed a hand through her brown hair only faintly tinged with gray. Her voice slowed with sadness. "You'll learn. It doesn't really pay to trust too much."

There was an uncomfortable pause. Thoughts of Kaler O'Connell were momentarily forgotten while everyone tried vainly not to think how Bud Trowbridge had de-

14

serted Harriet, just up and walked out after seventeen years of marriage. Beth alone did not dwell on Harriet's troubles. She was too busy fighting the familiar ache, the pain that had driven her back home. Harriet was right; she had been too trusting, but she'd already learned her bitter lesson. She knew only too well how disillusioning people could be. Lance had taught her that with complete thoroughness.

Martha, however, was not to be deterred for long. She liked nothing better than to feel superior to someone else, and there was a heady righteousness in feeling superior to those of O'Connell's stamp.

"That's true, Harriet, sadly true," she said, then pounced back to her original point. "And you can't trust an O'Connell at all. It's in the blood."

"Bad blood, those O'Connells," Patsy added, and a general shaking of heads followed.

"I can't remember seeing Jack O'Connell draw a single sober breath."

"Or do a day's honest work."

"What about that Essie? A fine mother she was, running off when her boy was no bigger than a grasshopper."

"Would you have stuck around with Jack? His temper was ugly and he was violent, a beater."

"Maybe not, but I wouldn't have left my baby behind," declared Sally fiercely.

Beth let the talk swirl around her, no longer eager to stem the flow. She'd wanted only to kindle a debate, not get caught up in the heat of it. She didn't know why she'd felt compelled to argue on Kaler O'Connell's behalf anyway. If she'd ever said a word to him in her life, she couldn't recall it. She couldn't remember anything about him at all actually. It had all been so many years ago. . . .

She leaned her head back and closed her eyes and saw vague visions of a darkly handsome youth with a defiant

15

look and a daredevil laugh. Yes, he'd been proud and wild and a loner. Always the one who didn't fit in. Always the one others talked about, always the town's bad boy. But the town's bad boy was all grown up now; let him fight his own battles.

What, she wondered idly, would the man be like?

Her eyes flew open. The muted lamplight cast shadowed crescents throughout the room, highlighting this face and shading the next. Every face she saw was as familiar to her as her own reflection in the mirror each morning. She'd known all of them all of her life and in a town the size of Pasque, that meant she knew their habits, their likes, their dislikes. She knew without asking that Harriet took sugar in her tea, but not in her coffee, that Ruth took sugar in, and on, everything, while Martha never took sugar at all. She knew that Patsy did laundry on Mondays, went to the beautician's on Fridays and shopped on Saturdays. She knew that Sally and her husband had been to see a specialist in Sioux Falls before Sally finally got pregnant. And she knew that each of them knew as much, and more, about her. It wasn't nosiness, it was simply the way of life in Pasque, South Dakota.

"When I grow up I'm going to go away from here and never come back," Beth had often cried as a child. It wasn't that she'd been unhappy; she'd grown up secure, accepted, loved. Looking back, her days seemed unbelievably full, crammed with schoolwork and chores and 4-H projects, clouded with sibling squabbles, lightened with loving laughter. Yes, she'd been happy growing up here. But Beth had craved anonymity, privacy, the luxury of being left alone, something she'd never received as the fourth of seven children in a town where every adult acted like another parent whenever hers happened to be unavailable. When she'd finally grown up, Beth had lived up to her childhood vow. She'd gone to college, and after

16

college she'd moved to Minneapolis and at first she'd loved it all. She'd loved the noise and the dirt and the constant traffic. She'd liked shouldering her way through a crowd of strangers, none of them knowing where she was going or why. She'd liked having a room of her own, where no one coughed in the night or shuffled about in the morning. She'd liked not having to share her every waking moment with someone else. At first, she'd loved it.

But in the end, Beth had come back to Pasque.

And now Kaler O'Connell had come back. With even less reason to—she, after all, had returned to the loving comfort of family and friends—he'd come back to Pasque.

It seemed to Beth that she was on the verge of making some significant correlation about all this when Candace interrupted her thoughts, ruffling the top of her blond head and demanding to know if Beth intended to see her guests out or not. Only then did Beth realize that everyone else was standing, smoothing out their summer skirts and blue jeans as they waited for her. She jerked out of the rocker, sending it whisking back and forth on the oak floor.

"I'm sorry," she said, smiling contritely. She led them through the hall to the heavy door with the oval glass that company and strangers used. Everyone else came in through the kitchen, banging the screen and calling out for Emma or Beth or Jenny. Anyone looking for the men went straight to the fields.

"Woolgathering, Beth?" asked Ruth.

"She must've been thinking about some man. Only a man can make a woman that dreamy in the middle of one of *our* meetings!" teased Sally, and laughter filed out with them into the summer night.

That contrariness of hers rose up again. Standing in a

17

stream of hazy porchlight, Beth said cheerily, "Matter of fact, I was. I was thinking of Kaler O'Connell."

The laughter stopped abruptly. Crickets choroused and moonlight glossed the white porch railing. "Now, Beth," reproved Harriet even as Candace whirled around and marched back. Near the top step she halted and peered up at Beth, her eyes narrowing against the yellow light. "What do you mean, you were thinking of O'Connell?"

"I was just wondering how he'll adjust," she answered with a shrug.

"What's going on, Beth? Was there something between you two all those years ago?"

"Who? Me?" squeaked Beth, startled out of her bedeviling mood. She gaped at Candace in amazement.

Her sister-in-law continued to regard her sternly, intent lines puckering around her brown eyes. "Yes, you. You and Kaler O'Connell."

"Of course not! How could you think such a thing? We didn't even know each other. I was just a kid back then, Candy. Honestly, he probably wouldn't know me from Myrtle Eisenberg's pet poodle."

"Then why are you so concerned about him?"

"I'm not. I was just . . ." She was at a loss how to explain herself. She couldn't really deny that she'd felt concerned; she had. She'd felt downright sorry for him. But not because she had any feelings for him, not any feelings of the kind Candy was implying at any rate. She cleared her throat and tried again. "I was just whipping up some debate, you know, playing the devil's advocate. The rest of you were agreeing like sheep and I thought I'd disagree to make the evening interesting."

"I hope that's all it is, Beth, for your sake. You don't want to get mixed up with him. A nice girl like you doesn't want to waste her time with a convict."

"*Ex*-convict," she amended before she could stop herself.

18

Worry flashed over Candace's full features. She glanced back at the women listening avidly to this exchange, and returned her uneasy gaze to Beth. She mounted another step. "Maybe I should talk with Mom and Dad Rasmussen. . . ."

Beth slid in front of the door, as if to block her way. "Don't be silly, Candy. I'm not mixed up with him; I'm not about to get mixed up with him; I've never been mixed up with him. Believe me, if I had, you'd have known about it. *Everybody* would've known about it."

Candace wavered. "You're sure?"

"Of course I'm sure. Around here, you can't sneeze without having everybody know about it."

"This isn't something to joke about!"

Beth offered a placating smile. "Sorry. But I can't help making fun of such a ridiculous situation. I don't even know him, except what's said about him, and I don't think I'll ever get to know him, so there's absolutely nothing for you to worry about, okay?"

For a moment more, Candace hovered uncertainly on the step. A car door slammed, then another. She checked the watch on her wrist, straightened, and shook a determined finger at Beth. "Okay. But don't waste any more of your time feeling sorry for him. A man like that makes his own trouble and there's no sense feeling sorry for him. All right?"

"All right," Beth agreed with a nod, but when she went back into the house she still felt a nagging sense of sorrow she didn't fully understand.

19

CHAPTER TWO

She saw that he didn't recognize her and wondered at the tiny stab of—what? Disappointment? She knew that was absurd. As she'd insisted so stoutly the week before, she'd hardly even known him. She'd been a real kid when he left; she couldn't seriously expect him to remember her. Would she have remembered him if he'd been just another face from the high school yearbook, instead of "that wild O'Connell boy" no one could forget?

They certainly hadn't forgotten. Town talk had been ample proof of that. Each disparaging remark had stirred her ever-ready sympathy for the underdog and was, she supposed now, why she'd felt compelled to see him. Of course, this interview would be nothing more than an empty gesture, but when Dee had announced, in a dramatic stage whisper, who was here wanting work, Beth simply hadn't been able to turn him away.

Sighing inwardly, she motioned him toward the straight-backed chair beside her cluttered desk. Running her hand over the creases in her apricot linen skirt, she took her own seat as he slid soundlessly into the chair. Even seated he seemed to dominate the cramped office, his shadow looming over her, blocking the already dim light. She fussed needlessly with a sheath of papers, wishing she'd not put herself in this unpleasant position. Finally she folded her hands over the top of the stack and looked at him.

Beth stared into guarded gray eyes and rapidly readjusted her thinking. She'd felt sorry for him, sorry for the years he'd wasted, sorry for the continual censure he had to endure. She'd felt a wave of pity when he'd entered wearing the same awful brown suit he'd worn the day of his arrival, with its baggy fit and sheen of age. She'd felt an even stronger wave when she'd seen how sharply gaunt his face had become, how much thinner he was than her memory of him. But looking now at that shuttered face, she realized her mistake. This man didn't need her pity. He didn't look as if he needed anything or anyone at all.

She glanced down at her hands. She should be inquiring about his background, but she knew his background —everybody did. She should be testing his attitude, but she knew his attitude and it wasn't the attitude she usually looked for in an applicant. No one else had thought him a suitable applicant; she'd heard of several area farmers who'd refused to hire him, and Leonard had disagreed strongly with her decision to see him today. Leonard was right, she shouldn't have agreed to interview him. But she had agreed to it and she needed to get on with it.

Unfolding her hands, she scanned his application and cleared her throat. "I see you worked in the library at the —uh, at the—"

"At the prison, yes."

She raised her eyes. His seemed to be focused on the catalogues and magazines spilling over the shelf behind her, yet she had the distinct, uncomfortable impression he was precisely aware of her least movement. Flustered, she dog-eared the corner of his application. "Though we publish books, I'm afraid library work really isn't much of a qualification for work here. We publish and sell craft books and kits."

"If you look further," he said with measured civility, "you'll see I worked in industry for a couple of years."

Slightly abashed, she obediently checked the form. "Yes, I see," she murmured. "Making shoes. You also worked on the yard?"

He nodded. "Maintenance, custodial work."

"Oh, I see," she repeated inanely.

"I'm willing to learn whatever I need to," he said after a pause. "I've been told I'm a quick learner."

"You never seemed much interested in learning back in school," she commented without thinking, remembering the brash bad boy of a decade ago.

Surprise passed through his eyes. She could see he hadn't expected her to make a remark like that. But how could he have? She hadn't expected it herself.

"We went to high school together," she explained quickly.

"There was a Rasmussen," he said. "But I thought her name was—"

"Marilyn," supplied Beth. "We weren't together exactly. You were in my sister Marilyn's class. I was three years behind, a freshman when you were a senior."

Now he openly studied her. His gaze traveled over her slowly, taking stock of each feature within her oval face, but without any of the masculine appreciation she normally received. She examined his expression as he made note of her eyes, her small, straight nose, her pale lips. It was like trying to read hieroglyphics; a message was there, but she couldn't decipher it.

"You don't look much like her," he finally remarked.

"No, I don't, do I? But then, I don't look much like anyone else in my family. I'm always told that. They're all more brown than blond and I'm more blond than brown and—" Beth stopped abruptly. She was babbling

22

nervously and she knew it. Worse, she knew he knew it too.

"Not blond," he corrected her. "Prairie gold."

She looked at him in bewilderment. "Come again?"

"Your hair. It's like prairie grass in August."

Almost of its own volition, her hand crept up to touch the sleek curls brushing her shoulder. Her fingers twirled within a few strands. Prairie gold. What an extraordinary thing for him to have said. She suddenly realized he was watching her intently and hastily dropped her hand.

The bare suggestion of a smile touched his mouth, unsettling her further. Well, this was more like the O'Connell she'd expected. The wolfish comment, the sly hint of sensuality on his lips. She straightened and sought to regain control of the interview. "Now, about your application—"

"You had a brother too. Chris or Charles or something."

She wavered, thinking she shouldn't let him call the shots. After all, she was the one in charge here. But that flicker of light behind the shutter drew a response she couldn't repress. "Charlie. He was a couple of years ahead of you."

"Played football," he said.

"Yes," she affirmed, no longer resisting being sidetracked. "And basketball and baseball and any other sport you could think of. Most of my siblings are sports nuts."

"There are others?"

Her mouth danced into a grin. "Seven of us."

"Seven!" He pursed his lips on a soundless whistle. "No wonder it always seemed like there were more Rasmussens than any other kids in town."

"But all seven of us put together never had the impact of one O'Connell."

Even as the words left her mouth, she regretted them.

23

But it was too late. The trace of warmth, as small as it had been, disappeared from his expression altogether. Beth felt as if a layer of ice had formed between them, crushing and freezing their rapport.

Knowing she must, she cleared her throat and got back to business. "You realize, Mr. O'Connell, that we're a very small company. Openings are very limited and at the moment—"

His chair slid back; he came to his feet. Beth bent back to gape up at him. A muscle tightening in his jaw was the only sign of his anger. His voice held no hint of emotion. "Unlike your brother Charlie, I'm not much for games, so let's end the charade. You can thank me now for my time and tell me my application will go on file and I can thank you for your time and leave, giving you the opportunity to toss it."

He reached the door in a single step. His hand closed over the knob and Beth catapulted from her chair. "Wait!"

Her request held the imperious ring of a command. His hand on the knob, he waited.

Beth knew she should have let him go, knew she should have felt relieved that he'd understood the situation. But she didn't feel relieved. She felt pain and anger and embarrassment. Most of all, she felt a renewal of unbearable pity that he'd so readily accept, even expect, rejection. She stared at his back, wanting to tell him how sorry she was, wanting to somehow ease his pain.

"All that's available is warehouse work," she said slowly, unwillingly. "Filling stock orders and loading trucks."

He said nothing. He didn't have to speak. His tense stance loudly declared his skepticism.

The room was shrinking in size. Beth could feel the steel file cabinets closing in on her from the left while the overfull shelf crowded her from behind. She couldn't pos-

24

sibly hire a man like O'Connell. What would people say? After a heartbeat of silence she moistened her dry lips.

"The pay wouldn't be much. Just over minimum, actually."

Turning with slow deliberation, he inquired coolly, "Are you offering me a job?"

His insolent stare issued the real challenge, daring her to admit she was doing nothing of the sort. It was the kind of cock-sure arrogance one expected from Kaler O'Connell, the kind of look and tone that inevitably set people's backs up.

Bristling, Beth drew a deep breath and did what she'd somehow known all along she would do. "Yes," she told him. "I am."

His insolence vanished like snow from a volcano. Tension radiated from him as he scrutinized her. But when he finally spoke, he spoke quietly. "You don't have to do this. You don't have to hire me out of pity."

She flinched, started to deny it, but met his gaze and said instead, "I happen to think you're capable of the work."

"I know I am. I intend to fully earn my pay wherever I work. But I don't want to be given misplaced charity."

O'Connell pride collided with Rasmussen obstinacy. His reluctance to accept the job only increased her determination that he should have it, even if she had to round him up and bring him in each and every day of the week. Without so much as glancing at him, Beth crossed briskly to the door. "There's a thirty-day probationary period," she stated purposefully, "at the end of which you'll be eligible for full company benefits and a raise. After that, wage reviews are January and June. If you'll follow me, I'll introduce you to the warehouse foreman."

Grasping the knob, her hand lightly brushed his arm. Her hair seemed to crackle, her scalp to tingle. She jerked back and her shoulder knocked against a cross-stitched

25

plaque hanging on the wall which proclaimed BETH RAS-MUSSEN, RESIDENT EXPERT. She could only hope he didn't notice how her hand trembled as she fumbled to straighten it.

Mustering what dignity she could, she strode out. She wasn't all that certain he would follow her bumbling exit. Within seconds she realized just how much she wanted him to follow. Her heart sank to new depths as she waited in the hall. Should she wait? Walk on? Go back and confront him?

He came out of her office looking cool and composed. "Show me the warehouse," he said.

They walked side by side down a concrete corridor that seemed narrower than usual to Beth. Each step resounded with a hollow slap that echoed the knocking of her heart. As much as she wanted to, she couldn't ignore the wild rhythm of her careening pulse. She told herself it wasn't the taut caution of his catlike movements. She told herself it wasn't the aura of strength, even danger, that emanated from him. If she felt like an overwound clock, her heart ticking frantically and her nerves tightly coiled, she assured herself it had nothing whatsoever to do with the man beside her.

She cast him a sidelong look. He unexpectedly met her glance with his own. Both quickly looked away.

It must be guilt, she concluded, and promptly fell victim to self-recriminations. My God, she'd hired him! How could she? Had she lost her mind? What would Nelda say to having an ex-convict working in her warehouse? Why did Nelda have to be in Minneapolis this week? Why couldn't he have waited until Nelda got back? Why . . .

Beth pulled herself up short. There was nothing to be gained from such thoughts. She'd done what she thought was best. Striving to regain her usual composure, she suc-

26

ceeded, at least, in maintaining the outward appearance of it as she began speaking in a breathy staccato.

"Nelda Evenson started Creative Crafts in her home less than eight years ago. As you can see, she's turned it into an impressive business. Around here, we like to say that Creative Crafts put Pasque on the map, and that's really not far from the truth. We do business all over the nation. Besides the books and kits, we sell all the fabrics and supplies necessary to make any item shown in one of our books. We deal mostly with hobby and craft stores, but have a growing list of individual orders as well. And of course, all the kits are custom designed."

As she finished her explanation, they arrived at a pair of double doors and she crossed in front of him to peer through the dirt-streaked window. A second later she thrust the door open and ushered him forward. Tiers and tiers of metal shelves with open bins formed aisles that checkered the hangarlike warehouse. Unseen forklifts rumbled in the distance, underscoring the hum of activity as people moved, busily shifting items from bins to boxes and from boxes to bins. Nothing ever quelled that unending hum, yet there was a murmur that followed their progress, like a missed beat in the company's pulse. Beth ignored it as she led Kaler to where two men in shirt-sleeves stood in a patch of light swirling with dustmotes.

"I have a new worker for you, Dutch," she said in greeting. "Kaler O'Connell just signed on."

The older man squinted at Kaler, pressing all the crinkles around his eyes into a new pattern. The younger one said, "O'Connell?" in a clearly shocked tone.

"That's right, Eddie," Beth confirmed a little too brightly. She turned slightly to Kaler. "Eddie Curran here is assistant foreman, while Dutch Vandervelde's our head foreman and most indispensable employee."

"Tell many more like that and your nose'll be too long

27

for your face," laughed Dutch in a low rumble that faintly resembled an idling forklift.

She laughed, too, and began to relax. Dutch teased her only when he was in a good mood. It was his way of letting her know he accepted her decision to hire Kaler as a good one. Even Eddie's obvious disapproval couldn't dent her newfound cheer. "I'll leave Kaler with you, Dutch, while I take care of the paperwork with Leonard. You can show him around, explain a bit about his job and hours. He starts . . ." She paused, looked questioningly at Kaler. "Tomorrow?"

"Tomorrow's fine," he said.

"Good. We'll see you tomorrow then." She pivoted and walked out of the warehouse with a pert spring to her step. She'd cleared the first hurdle with room to spare. Dutch hadn't raised so much as an eyebrow. Once on the other side of the double doors, she stopped. After the briefest hesitation, she gave in to the urge to look back.

Through the streaks on the windowpane she watched as Kaler removed his brown suitcoat. He folded it neatly and draped it over his arm with a precision that pleased her. She was a very precise person herself. Not, of course, that that had anything to do with anything.

Even at this distance she could see how much better he looked without his old jacket. She could see he was in excellent shape; his arms and chest were well developed and more muscled than she'd have imagined. Not, of course, that she'd imagined anything at all about his muscles, but still he'd looked so thin. . . .

"Are you thinking of cleaning it?" inquired someone behind her.

Beth jumped and whirled around in one motion, her hand flying to her chest and her mouth popping open. "Leonard!" she squeaked.

"I didn't know you did windows," he said, seeming to

tease Beth but failing in the attempt. He wasn't a man who knew how to give or accept a good-natured joke. She knew he really meant, Why are you standing around when you should be working? Her confidence waned. He certainly wouldn't think she'd made the right decision about O'Connell. Far from it.

Squaring her shoulders, she met his accusation with one of her own. "You scared me, sneaking up on me like that."

He glanced from her guilt-stricken face to the window and back again. He took a step forward and surveyed the scene through the window. When he turned to face her, she saw a wealth of disapproval, compounded by disbelief, settle over his long, thin face.

"Don't tell me you hired him. You could not have hired him," he stated with conviction. Leonard always backed his statements with conviction. He was assured, opinionated, a perfectionist who never doubted that he knew what was best. Beth usually went out of her way to avoid disagreeing with him because arguing with him was like arguing with a brick wall. He held an opinion and didn't budge from it. This time, however, she had no intention of backing away from a confrontation.

"On the contrary, Leonard, I not only can, I have."

"Are you telling me you've actually made Kaler O'Connell an employee of this company?"

"Yes."

"A convict, a criminal?"

"That was before," she began, but stopped at the disgusted huff that Leonard emitted.

"Do you think eight years in prison made a choirboy out of O'Connell? If you think he's changed, you're more naive than I'd thought. A leopard doesn't change his spots."

"How could he not be changed? He's not the wild boy everyone remembers. He's not an impulsive teenager anymore. He's twenty-eight and Lord knows that would be change enough." She thought of how he'd told her she didn't have to give him the job and added with emphasis, "The man I interviewed bore very little resemblance to that kid. He was open and sincere."

As if the sight of her offended him, Leonard removed his black-rimmed glasses and carefully cleaned them with his handkerchief. He returned his glasses to his nose, shook out the square of linen, then replaced it in his back pocket. "I knew," he said finally, funereally, "you shouldn't have seen him. Despite your assurance that you wouldn't offer him a job, I knew you'd end up feeling sorry for him and give him one. You're the type of woman who can't pass by a stray puppy."

He made it sound as if this marked her as a tainted woman. She thrust up her chin. "Nonsense. It's nothing like that."

"Isn't it? If you didn't feel sorry for him, why did you hire him?"

Why indeed? She couldn't deny it; she *had* felt sorry for him and she had hired him for that very reason. Even Kaler had realized as much. But she couldn't admit it. To do so would seem like a betrayal of Kaler. She temporized, saying, "Someone has to give him a chance."

"Nelda should be the one to decide whether or not this company took such a risk."

He was no longer attacking O'Connell, but her judgment. Some of the strain she felt abated. She was on surer ground, defending herself rather than the man everyone else loved to hate, and she responded with more assurance. "Nelda hired me to make those decisions for her. There's no guarantee that all my decisions will be the right ones, but even if I'm wrong, you aren't in the position to object, Leonard. The decision was my responsibility, not yours."

He opened his mouth, evidently thought better of

speaking, and shut it again. He ran a hand over his thinning brown hair, eyeing her consideringly from behind the thick lenses of his glasses. It wasn't often that someone stood up to Leonard, and it was easy to see that he didn't like it. A thread of amusement lightened Beth's mood, but she took care to conceal it. Her amusement, she knew, would only annoy him further.

"I hope you don't come to regret it," he said at last.

"So do I," she said with complete truth.

The discussion ended, for the time being at least, and they left the warehouse area. Try as she might not to, Beth couldn't help recalling how when Kaler walked beside her, the corridor had seemed narrower and her blood had pulsed to the rhythm of his movement. Her pulse began to beat now, throbbing with an intensity that disturbed her. His shadow seemed to haunt her, and though she felt foolish, she couldn't keep from looking over her shoulder. The hall was empty.

She halted beside her door. "Can you get Kaler O'Connell's forms ready? He starts work in the morning."

"Of course," Leonard said tightly, and she knew he would. The one thing about Leonard that no one could deny was that he did his job and did it well. It was, in Beth's opinion, the one thing that made him tolerable. Before she could escape, Leonard threw in a last word. "I'll save myself some time and fill out the unemployment records as well."

"You do that," she sighed, and slipped into her office.

It wasn't the sanctuary she'd longed for. She couldn't flee from the thoughts that battered her mind. Sinking into her chair, propping her head in her hands, she accepted the pummeling of her censorious thoughts.

What if Leonard were right? What if she'd been naive and trusting, hiring O'Connell for all the wrong reasons? Even though she could see he'd changed, he hadn't exactly become Mr. Personality. He was an enigma. For all

31

she knew, he might be casing the joint or whatever it was robbers did, planning the next heist. A man like that makes his own troubles, Candace had said, but what if he made trouble for her?

She lifted her head and dropped her hands to the desk with a ringing slap of her palms. Whatever her reasons for hiring him, she'd made her decision and she'd stick by it. And really, he wasn't totally unsociable. He'd told her, hadn't he, that her hair was like a golden prairie?

CHAPTER THREE

A subtle, flowery fragrance lingered even after the double doors had swung shut. Kaler tried to ignore the scent, tried to ignore the stirrings he felt. But after so many years in a world without women, the perfume tantalized him. He wondered what it would be like to immerse himself in the sweetness of it, in the soft, clean sweetness of her.

Throughout the interview he'd been vividly, painfully, aware of her, of the crisp sway of her apricot skirt, of the shapely curve of her legs, of her delicate femininity. His response had been immediate and sharp. He managed to suppress the achings. He was well practiced in the denial of his physical needs, but he'd done so only with difficulty. He had never before had to overcome the added allure of a woman's charm.

She had charmed him all right. She'd charmed him with her kindness, her nervousness, and even with the strength he'd seen in her fine-boned features. She'd charmed him into making that asinine observation about her hair. She'd charmed him into reminiscing about the old days. She'd charmed him into talking, thinking like a regular person. He had been so charmed, in fact, that for a few precious minutes he'd almost forgotten who and what he was.

But she'd brought him back to earth with a jolt, reminding him exactly who he was. O'Connell, the social outcast.

He'd seen the pity cloud her blue eyes. He'd heard the reluctance in her voice. He'd seen and heard enough to know just why she hadn't wanted to give him a job and just why she had. He'd come to the brink of telling her to take her job and her pity and go to hell. But some shred of sanity overpowered his pride and he'd kept silent.

Bit by bit relief seeped in. He savored it, lingering over the delicious taste of it. He had a job. Unbelievably, he had a job. And with it he had the start to the new life he intended to make for himself.

All he wanted, all he'd dreamed about and longed for, was to fade into the normality of life, to work at a steady job, to buy clothes and food, to pay bills and taxes, just slip into the current of life unconfined by walls. That's all he wanted, all he needed. He didn't expect anything more. He didn't intend to grasp for the brass ring, not this time around.

It was obvious that the foreman and the younger man were surprised that Beth had hired him and even more so that the younger one, the one called Eddie, was displeased. He relaxed a little more. He knew how to deal with Eddie; he'd dealt with the Eddies of the world all his life. As for the older one, Kaler liked what he saw. He figured he'd get a fair shake. If he did his job, he'd have no trouble from Dutch.

"Take care of these orders," Dutch now said to Eddie, "while I show young O'Connell here around."

Eddie visibly hesitated before taking the proffered clipboard and stamping off. Not seeming to notice his assistant's ire, Dutch began outlining the scope of Kaler's duties, which mostly entailed filling shipment orders and loading them onto a truck. As he listened, Kaler looked around the warehouse, instinctively noting the dark corners, the blind spots most likely to lead to trouble. He didn't seem to realize yet that he didn't need to note them. He did it as naturally as he breathed, perhaps even more so.

They toured the rest of the warehouse, ducking into the glassed cubicle Dutch called his office that looked to Kaler more like a littered telephone booth. Notes were scattered over a bulletin board, pinned one atop another in seemingly haphazard fashion, and reams of colored paper—pink shipping sheets, blue lading bills, green order forms—smothered the black desktop. Totally unlike *her* office which, though equally small and cramped, had been neat, clean, even homey, with all the little touches she had added. The ivy plant on the shelf, the needlework hangings, the stone ladybug paperweight—it had all seemed so unbearably feminine.

"Looks like hell," said Dutch, cutting into Kaler's thoughts like a well-honed scalpel, "but there's a definite order in all this disorganization."

Kaler shot him a startled, defensive look. He saw the foreman's grin and realized Dutch was making small talk. Small talk, my God. He might as well be speaking in a foreign language. Maybe once, in another lifetime, Kaler had been able to engage in that sort of idle conversation, but his ability to do so had long since rusted. That he'd done so with *her* had been an inexplicable aberration, an unguarded instance he didn't intend to repeat. A glimmer of understanding passed through Dutch's eyes; he turned abruptly and held open the door. They continued the tour in silence.

Like the spare, concrete corridor, the employee lounge had a drab look Kaler could relate to. Vending machines, a few tables, and metal folding chairs drearily filled the area. A pay phone hung on the wall between the two rest rooms. The only attempt to lighten the dingy room was a yellow poster that read GOT A COMPLAINT? PLEASE

USE THIS FORM with an arrow indicating an infinitesimal square.

On the loading dock the forklifts droned beside them in a seemingly endless procession of loading and unloading. The sun slanted fully over the concrete, flooding them in warmth. Past the parking lot, beyond the daubing of cars, a field of wild grass stretched like an expansive, open sea. Kaler watched the grass bending in the wind and knew that later he would have the pleasure of walking through it. The knowledge intoxicated him.

"Well, that's about it," said Dutch. He, too, looked out over the field. "Any questions?"

"No, not yet."

"See you at eight tomorrow then."

He nodded and Dutch disappeared back into the maze of the warehouse. Kaler stood motionless. A sense of unreality grasped him. The grass undulated and beckoned and he wondered if it was a mirage, another tantalizing dream from which he'd jolt awake at any moment, the image shattering into fragments of tormented yearning. His stomach clenched and he almost longed for the familiarity of his old cell. It was all so different out here, so frighteningly different.

Ten days ago his physical world had been limited by stone walls and steel bars, a cheerless world of thick air clogged with stale odors, a tedious, colorless routine, an unending monotony twisted by the constant threat of explosive violence. The changing multitude of sights and smells now flooded his senses, until he feared he'd drown in the overwhelming fulfillment of it.

Funny how you could want something so badly, long for it with every fiber of your being, yet feel your gut tighten with fear when you finally got it. Year after year he'd dreamed of nothing but coming home. He'd envisioned it a thousand times, he'd almost tasted the joy of it, the sweet joy of freedom, of home. But on that first walk down Main Street, joy hadn't touched him. Fear, frustration, and bitterness, too, had roiled within him. Looking around, he'd realized with shock that the town he'd remembered so vividly in dream after dream had altered. He hadn't really expected it to be the same after so many years, yet the small changes disturbed him in ways he hadn't foreseen. Bea's Coffee Shop had become a pizza parlor, the old pool hall was now a video arcade. Hell, he'd never even played a video game! Each change seemed to signify a loss of time he'd never be able to recapture.

He felt the same tumbling of emotions now. With all his heart he'd wished for a chance to prove himself, a chance to prove that he'd changed. Well, he'd been granted his wish. He had a job; he had a chance to make good. And fear wrenched at him. An O'Connell make good? That was a laugh. The odds were against it, the deck stacked from the day of his birth. He had been set apart long before he even understood what it meant. But from the time he was old enough to realize what was expected of him, Kaler had done his best to live up to people's expectations, fulfilling his role as the town's bad boy with dedicated thoroughness. Once or twice he'd met with unexpected kindness—the candy store lady, who'd sometimes given him two when he could only afford one, the third-grade teacher who'd paid for his new sneakers out of her own pocket—but such confusing deeds were fleeting. By the time he was in high school, Kaler's fate had been sealed. He was, after all, an O'Connell.

Yet something within Kaler fiercely rejected this. He'd made a mess of his life, he admitted that, but the past was behind him. The future lay ahead, unblemished. If he'd learned one lesson in all the years of soul-searching, he had learned that he and he alone controlled his own destiny. If it meant swallowing his pride, suppressing his anger, stretching his abilities to their utmost limits, he would do it. He was determined to make a good life for himself.

The knot twisting his stomach loosened. He pivoted on his heel and wound his way back through the warehouse. Eddie and another man lounged near the double doors, talking. They stopped speaking as he walked by and he shoved with extra force, feeling a release in the loud *whoosh* of the doors. There was a wonderment, a sense of power in not having to wait for the doors to slide slowly open at someone else's command.

In something this small did he finally feel he'd regained control of his life.

Practicing a restraint she hadn't known she possessed, Beth stayed sequestered in her office. Though she was eager to know how her protégé was doing, she knew better than to fuss around Dutch's domain. She cudgeled her brain, but couldn't produce a legitimate excuse for doing so. Without that excuse all she'd do was cause talk and trouble. She wistfully eyed her phone, hoping vainly for a call from an irate customer whose shipment hadn't been received. The call never came; she stayed in her office.

An abundance of work, more than enough to fill her morning, should have kept her occupied. Proofs for two books of gingham-track patterns needed to be read, a fabric supplier had to be contacted and sweet-talked, the vacation schedule lay in front of her ready to be confirmed and posted. All of this should have made her morning fly, but instead, time trudged along. Minutes plodded like hours and as each dragged by, Beth found it more difficult to attend to her work. She checked the clock with increasing regularity and even once phoned "Time" to verify its accuracy. She felt restless, trapped.

Her impatience was heightened by her inability to take action. Beth liked to do things. She detested having to wait for anything. Feeling stymied, unable to march into the warehouse and demand to know how Kaler was doing, her mind began traveling in circles, returning to the game of second-guessing she'd played most of the night.

Had she taken leave of her senses? It seemed to be the general consensus, even among her family. Her younger brothers, Dale and Ted, had bluntly told her she'd been a "typical woman," thinking with her heart instead of her head. Teenaged Jenny had been even less help, declaring she thought it romantic. "You know, like *Shane,*" she'd expanded, her voice carrying with the stridency of one used to speaking over music blasting full volume. "He's all alone, with everyone against him, except *you,* you gave him a chance. I think it's noble," she'd ended on a drawn-out sigh. Beth had cringed.

But it had been her parents' silent concern that disturbed her the most. She'd carried their silence up to bed with her, worrying over it as she had not done over the critical remarks and censorious looks she'd received from others.

Beth had been blessed. Frank and Emma Rasmussen were loving and giving parents; their opinion meant a great deal to her. Though all grown up, a full quarter of a century old, she still felt the need for their approval. Even if she'd not seen the flash of concern pass between them, the very fact that they'd not expressed an opinion on her action would have told her they disapproved. She could ignore the criticism of the Leonard Smoltens and the Martha Hansons; their objections stemmed from the type of blind prejudice Beth could neither understand nor accept. But her parents weren't like that. If they thought she'd made a mistake, they had good reason for thinking so. A sadness blanketed her, stifling her in the still summer night.

She lay awake, regretful, cursing her impulsiveness and wishing she'd not hired him. Already he was fulfilling

Candy's dire prophesy and causing trouble. Throughout her fitful night the question had battered her: *why* had she done it?

Unfortunately morning brought no answer. She didn't know why she'd given O'Connell a job. Contrary to what her siblings had intimated, the last thing she'd thought of was romance. Leonard had been right; she'd felt sorry for him, but in the light of a new day that hardly seemed enough of a justification. Her coworkers at Crafts clearly thought she'd lost her mind; she'd seen it in their hurried glances, heard it in their hushed whispers. Maybe they were right. Perhaps her train had slipped off the track. The more she thought about it, the more likely an explanation it seemed. Why else would she have hired Kaler O'Connell?

She was tired of thinking about it; she was getting a headache. Her gaze again skimmed over the clock. The hands finally inched straight up and she escaped thankfully to the lounge and her lunch.

As she entered, conversation ceased. The chill of unpopularity iced her skin. She knew it would pass, but knowing didn't make it any easier to greet her coworkers. Dee and Janet shifted awkwardly on their chairs, Lisa looked away. Eddie took off his baseball cap, swiped his hand through his matted chestnut hair, and replaced it before giving her a terse nod. Several others let their eyes slide past hers without recognition. She fixed her attention on the sandwich machine.

The selections all looked the same, uniformly cellophane wrapped and unappetizing. She placed a fingertip on a button, then paused. Another shiver danced lightly over her. The tingly sensation was quite different from the cold animosity she'd felt before. She cast a sidelong look over her shoulder.

He was sitting alone, well away from those gathered

around the tables. His face was devoid of any expression; he looked not at her, but at the coffee cup in his hands.

Her heart thudding, she returned her regard to the sandwiches. She tried to focus on them, but her eyes refused to cooperate. They were filled with the image of Kaler's set face. She shoved a handful of coins into the machine and pressed a button at random.

Salami. She hated salami. With a moue of distaste she plucked the sandwich from the tray. A burst of laughter brought her head up. Eddie was waving his hands, immersed in some tale, as the trio of women listened with smiles of enjoyment. Her annoyance with the salami transferred instantly to them. They should feel ashamed, ignoring Kaler so blatantly, treating him like an outcast. He wasn't a social pariah!

She stole another peek at the far corner. How could they ignore him, when his presence charged the very air with a new electricity? His eyes met hers once briefly. She averted her gaze quickly, and immediately chided herself. What if he thought he'd offended her just by catching her eye? She pumped more coins into the soda machine and tapped her foot impatiently while it whirred and the can tumbled out. The rest of them might have less manners than her father's hogs, but she, at least, had been reared to behave more kindly. Collecting her cola, she spun and crossed purposefully to where he sat.

Surprise shot through him as he watched her approach. He tensed, unable to look away. The slit in her straight buff skirt whispered discreetly apart with each step, exposing a hint of shapely thigh. Even that small hint was enough to stir his imagination. After so many years with nothing but his own mind for stimulation and release, his imagination was incredibly forceful, uncomfortably so. He dropped his gaze and focused his thoughts on the stiff denim of his new jeans. She stopped in front of him. He finished his coffee and crushed the paper cup in his fist before finally looking at her. The corners of her mouth wavered in a tentative smile.

"So how's it been going?" Her voice cracked slightly.

"Fine," he said.

"Good. Good." She paused. "That's good," she said again, and fell into silence.

They watched each other, neither speaking, neither moving. Beth began to wish she'd eaten the hated salami and gotten out of here. She could feel the imprint of everyone else's stare upon her back, and, worse, the suffocating expectation that hung in the air. It was clearly too late to leave. With all of them observing her so intently, she had to say something, do something.

She cleared her throat. "Do you mind if I sit here?"

He stared at her for a long moment, long enough for her heart to sink all the way to her shoes. Why hadn't she left well enough alone? He flicked his eyes to the vacant chair beside him. Then he reached out and wiped the seat with his shirt-sleeve.

It was so unexpected, so curiously quaint, that Beth didn't feel as if she could take a breath or move a muscle, much less actually sit down. When she continued to stand immobile, he said, "If you don't sit, I'll have dirtied my sleeve for nothing."

He was teasing, actually teasing! It affected her in ways she couldn't begin to explore. With every nerve jangling like a firehouse bell, Beth sat on the dusted chair. "Thank you," she said, and instantly wished she'd sounded more cordial than prim.

"Thank you," he said in return.

She swung her gaze to meet his. He was regarding her with admiration and an indefinable something else. "Why thank me?" she asked.

"For having the courage to sit with me," he said simply, and the fire bell clanged in her ears.

"Don't be silly. It doesn't take courage to sit with you.

42

Besides, I never do anything courageous. I just wanted to find out how things have been going your first day on the job."

There was no way for him to express the fears, the joys, the raw tangle of emotions, he'd been feeling. He shifted. "Okay. Things have been okay."

"Good." She reached down to pick up her napkin, which had fallen to the floor, a hand away from his tan canvas shoes. Unlike the jeans, they were well-worn. Wondering at why she'd even notice, much less care, she yanked the cellophane from the sandwich and rattled, "Rotten lunch facilities, I almost never eat here. What did you have?"

He held up the mangled cup. "Coffee."

The salami remained an inch from her mouth. She gawked at him from over the bread. "That's it? Coffee? Didn't you have a sandwich or even a roll to go with it?"

"Just coffee." He settled his gaze somewhere in the vicinity of her shoulder. "I'm watching the budget until I get that first paycheck."

She dropped her eyes to the bread in her hand, then thrust it toward him. "Here. Take this. I'll get something else."

"No, I—"

"I insist. You have to eat something. You can't skip a meal when you're working so hard. Besides, you'd be doing me a favor. Really. I hate salami. It was a mistake, I punched the wrong button. Here. Now I'll get a ham and cheese. And would you like another coffee?"

He was left holding the salami. She'd scooped up her coin purse and darted back to the machines before he could even blink. He knew she was just being kind, sharing with him this way, but such kindness was foreign to him. It had been so long since anyone had cared whether he missed a meal or not, he didn't quite know how to accept it now.

She returned, handing him another cup of coffee and grinning widely. "I got the last ham sandwich. You don't know how grateful I am to you. I absolutely detest salami." She started to sit, but halted in mid-motion. She stared at the uneaten sandwich he still held and her grin vanished. She cast him a look so stricken, it was comical. "Don't *you* like salami either?"

Even if he hadn't, even if eating it would have given him hives, Kaler would have denied it. As it was, he refuted this with complete truth. "Salami's fine."

"Are you sure?" she demanded.

"I'm sure. In fact, it's one of my favorites." She continued standing, a mulish expression he was beginning to recognize coming over her pretty face. Any minute now she'd probably whirl and march to the machines to get him another sandwich, one more to his liking. Slowly, starting at the corners and gradually working inward, his mouth tilted into a smile. "Stop gawking and sit down. A man can't eat when he's being stared at."

That crooked curve of his lips dazzled her. It transformed him completely. Years washed away, distrust dissolved, severity vanished. Beth managed to plop down just as he took a huge bite of the sandwich. They ate in silence, both aware they were being keenly observed. Subdued bits of conversation drifted over them and Beth struggled to find something to say. But she couldn't tell him how breathtaking she found his smile; she couldn't tell him how much better, how much younger and more fit he looked in the jeans and blue work shirt. As she wiped the last crumbs from her lips, she decided work was the most appropriate topic.

"So, do you think you'll like the work here?"

"I'd like working anywhere the air smelled free," he said.

She tossed a startled look his way. She wanted to say something deep and meaningful, something to let him

44

know how much she was touched by him. All she managed was another inane, "Good," which sounded so hollow and stupid to her ears, she decided she'd do best to excuse herself and leave. She started to rise, but happened to glimpse Eddie's face. He glared at Kaler with unmistakable hostility. Annoyed, she turned a bright smile to Kaler. "I'm certain you'll like it even more once you've gotten used to the routine. And, of course, once everyone's gotten used to you."

His long lashes lowered. He studied her from beneath them. For no logical reason her heart began to thump irregularly.

"You mean once they've gotten used to an ex-con?" he asked on a drawl that held a tinge of menace. Or perhaps it was a twinge of pain.

Her brows drew together. She searched his expression, trying to decipher what it was exactly his tone had conveyed. His eyes were carefully void, his mouth an indefinable line, his cheekbones angularly set. She would not discover the answer that way; he was closed to her.

"Yes, I suppose in a way I do mean that," she said slowly. His jaw tightened and her heart twisted. "But what I really mean is once they've realized you're more than that, once they've gotten to know you as a person, things'll even out."

His distrust was plain for her to see. He didn't believe her and she didn't know how to convince him. She didn't know why it was so important to her that he believe in her, but it was important, heartstoppingly important, that she make him believe.

"Kaler, I realize it isn't easy for you; I know it can't be. But try to understand that it's not easy for us either. You've got to give us a little time—"

"I've done my time," he cut in, his voice edged with pain.

She drew in a sharp breath. He saw the hurt cross her

features and cursed himself for it; he saw the pity that immediately followed and cursed her for that.

Chairs scraped back, grating against the silence between them. One by one, the other diners ambled away, leaving the echoes of their chatter. Beth watched Eddie hover by the candy machine, willing him not to go, but he stayed only long enough to enjoy a seductive swish of Lisa's departing ponytail. They were alone.

Beth counted each frantic beat of her heart, trying to find something to say amid the tumbling of embarrassment and compassion she felt. At length, she forced herself to look at him. His austere expression didn't invite apologies or commiserations. But she had to say something; she couldn't go on sitting here like a lump of lead. She moistened her lips with the tip of her tongue and saw his eyes follow the motion. Her pulse quickened; she looked away. After an eternal moment she jerked to her feet. "I guess I should get back to work."

"Wait."

She hesitated. He swept the room with a glance, bringing his gaze finally to rest on her. He had no idea what to say. He just knew he couldn't let her walk out on such a negative note.

"Yes?" she prompted.

Rising, he stood next to her. She tipped her head to look up at him. His black hair, which was feathered over his brow, glowed with a silky sheen. She saw his pulse beating furiously against his temple and felt an urge to soothe it with her fingertips. She took a step back, away from him, away from his magnetic force.

Kaler read rejection in her hasty movement. Nothing in his life had ever seemed as important as regaining her acceptance, and he spoke with quiet urgency. "I'm sorry. After so much time waiting, I guess I've gotten impatient. I know acceptance won't come easily, from them or from me."

46

"From you?"

"It's not easy for me to accept being an ex-con," he admitted. Before she could give way to another burst of pity, he smiled unevenly and said lightly, "Anyway, I never did thank you yesterday for the job."

Like sunshine spilling from behind clouds, her smile suddenly brightened the room. "Oh, you needn't thank me for that."

"I want to. I want you to know I appreciate what you've done for me."

"I haven't done anything. It's what you'll do that matters."

"But you've given me the chance."

Happiness gripped her, squeezing until it was almost painful. It crushed the breath from her, and Beth didn't have enough left to speak another word. It was just as well. She wouldn't have known what to say anyway. Giving him another smile, she again turned to leave.

"And Miss Rasmussen," he said, halting her.

She looked over her shoulder. Her heart nearly stopped. His eyes were flashing like quicksilver.

"I won't let you down," he said.

She somehow managed to make her wobbly legs walk.

CHAPTER FOUR

The irate customer called a week later. As was usual in the case of missing shipments, Beth transferred the call to Dutch. As was not usual, she followed it up with a personal visit to his office. Because, as usual, he wasn't there, she went in search of him through the labyrinth of the warehouse.

Though her view was partially blocked by bolts of cloth stacked on a crate platform, she had no trouble locating the foreman. His silvery hair stood out like a beacon in the dim light and she strode forward, passing a half dozen pickers taking hoops, fabrics, and trims out of bins and putting them into boxes for shipment. As she'd known it would, the chilly reserve was melting and she received several friendly greetings along the way.

"Morning, Dutch," she called as she neared.

He nodded absently, continuing to mark an inventory sheet pinned to a clipboard. Knowing better than to interrupt him, she waited quietly, letting her eyes wander. She wasn't consciously searching through the warehouse canyons, yet there was a definite sense of accomplishment when her gaze came to rest on Kaler.

His back to her, unaware of her presence, he removed a strapped box from a heavy-duty scale, marked the weight on the top, and shoved it aside. He lifted another onto the scale. His muscles shifted beneath his shirt, the cream material bunching and smoothing with each motion. There was certainly nothing in that to make her heart patter like rain on a tin roof, but her heart pattered just the same.

He paused to swipe his arm across his brow. Sweat dampened the back of his shirt, glistened on his arm. Even in repose there was no mistaking the strength of those arms. What would it be like to be wrapped within the powerful circle of such arms? Her mouth went dry with the thought of it.

"Beth," said Dutch.

She returned to reality with a jolt. She swung her startled gaze to the foreman. As she focused on him she realized he'd spoken to her and had the sinking feeling it hadn't been the first time. Embarrassment was quickly chased by a bristling irritation. What was the matter with her? She was acting like a moonstruck fool!

"What brings you back into the warehouse?" Dutch asked a shade impatiently.

She could see he'd consider talking with her a waste of time, but now that she was here, she had to say something. She plunged in. "I just wondered if you'd solved yesterday's problem—the lost order for Billie's Craft Emporium. Did you ever find out what happened?"

If Dutch thought her inquiry odd, he didn't show it. "The order never got out of the warehouse. We didn't have a pink slip on it and I was about to chew Smolten's a— tell Smolten to find out what had happened when O'Connell found the slip stuck beneath one of the platforms."

Involuntarily her gaze veered to Kaler. He worked with an economy of motion, a supple strength that mesmerized her. How long she stared at him, she didn't know, but it was long enough for the silence to strike her, long enough for her to realize Dutch had followed the direction of her stare. He was eyeing Kaler with speculation and she cringed mentally.

"O'Connell found the slip, you said?" she asked with what she hoped was nonchalance.

He shot her a sharp look. "Yeah. It must've fallen off a pile and slid behind the platform. Just one of those things that happens. Nelda had us ship out an extra carton of kits, gratis, to make up for it. The whole load went out this morning."

"Well, I'm glad it all got straightened out." She knew she should leave; she'd used up her meager excuse, but still she lingered. Dutch, too, waited, seeming to expect something more. Feeling awkward, unsure in a way she'd not felt since adolescence, she finally brought herself to ask, "How's he doing, by the way?"

Dutch didn't pretend not to understand. "Does his job and keeps to himself."

She could have shaken him until his false teeth fell out. She wanted details, descriptions, something to point to and say, See? I told you he'd make it. Instead, Dutch gave her a laconic pat on the head.

"Still, in a week, you must've seen whether or not he does a good job," she prompted.

"Good enough."

She gave up. You couldn't pry anything out of Dutch Vandervelde he didn't want you to have anyway. Saying she was glad the snafu with Billie's had been straightened out, she left him. Threading her way along the aisles of towering shelves, she decided her short visit hadn't been totally wasted. At least she could be buoyed by the fact that Kaler was doing okay. "Good enough" was about as much praise as anyone could expect from Dutch.

"Keeps to himself," he'd also said. She didn't have to wonder what that meant. Given the sample of the one lunch she'd taken in the lounge, she could be fairly certain that the others were still ignoring him. She could only guess at this because she hadn't had the courage to return to the lounge after that day. It was too risky. He'd disturbed her too much and in ways she didn't want to examine too closely.

Her lips began to tighten. She was being absurd. All they'd done was talk a bit. And really, if she wanted to know how Kaler was doing, she should simply ask him. She was behaving foolishly, avoiding him. He might even misinterpret it. After all, there was no doubt about why everyone else avoided him. Beth halted in her tracks. No, she wasn't going to treat him the way everyone else did. People made mistakes, she knew that only too well, and she wasn't going to condemn his future along with his past, not unless she had reason to do so.

She straightened the skirt of her pastel print dress and combed her fingers through her hair. She would simply ask him how he was, chat a bit, and then get back to work. Breathing in deeply, she retraced her steps.

"Good morning, Kaler," she said, and congratulated herself on her level tone.

He spun around, wary surprise crossing his face. It passed swiftly, leaving a guarded pleasure. "Morning, Miss Rasmussen."

"Please, call me Beth. We're not that formal; we're all on a first-name basis here."

He nodded, but he didn't say it. A few seconds thudded by, seconds in which she learned just how much she'd have liked to have heard her name on his lips. He leaned against the scale, his pose deceptively casual. She knew the pose was misleading; nothing about him was ever casual. Not daring to ask herself why, she wished she could erase his tension. . . .

"Dutch says your work's good enough," she finally said. "Coming from Dutch, that's high praise indeed."

"I'm glad to hear it. I think a lot of Dutch's opinion."

"We all do." She waited, hoping he'd say something

51

more. When he didn't, she shuffled the toe of her shoe over the bare concrete and gathered her courage together. "Maybe we could have lunch again sometime," she suggested in a voice disgustingly squeaky. To cover her embarrassment, she added, "You owe me one."

"Sounds good," he said.

There was an unconvincing quality about his agreement. Beth wanted to press him, name a day, and commit him to it, but she sensed his discomfort and let it drop. Saying good-bye, she was about to move on when she caught sight of two pickers watching her with intent interest. They exchanged a comment and the blatant derision in their expressions nettled her. Her voice crackled with emotion as she impulsively exclaimed, "Kaler, I'm sorry for the way they're all behaving."

He gaped at her with open incredulity. He couldn't imagine anyone feeling that much emotion on his behalf, especially not someone like Beth. She was so obviously everything he wasn't, so good, so unblemished. "You don't have to apologize for anything," he started, but she interrupted fiercely.

"Yes, I do! They haven't the manners to do it, so I will. It's shameful the way they ignore you."

Too many emotions were being stirred by her outburst. He'd worked at being insensate for so long, he didn't know how to handle such feelings. Normally he'd resist them with an aloof indifference, but he couldn't even pretend indifference to her. Mustering a reasonably light tone, he contradicted her. "But I haven't been ignored."

She cast him a look of disbelief that changed instantly to one of sheer fury. "If anyone's been harassing you—"

"No, I didn't mean anything like that," he broke in quickly. "All I meant was they've been watching me, not ignoring me. Most days, I've practically had my own shadow."

"Shadow?" she echoed.

"I think his name's Leonard."

One of his lopsided smiles lifted the corners of his mouth, beguiling her into forgetting her fuming indignation. When he looked at her like that, it was a wonder she could remember her own name.

"I'd call him something a whole lot less polite than a shadow," she retorted with a grin, and had the pleasure of hearing him chuckle.

"But you're a lady, so you'll courteously refrain from doing so," he teased.

Her smile weakened. She wasn't such a lady, but she couldn't bear the thought of him knowing it. She could scarcely bear admitting it to herself. He might be able to openly bear the stigma of his past—it was one of the things she most admired about him—but she couldn't, not yet, at least. As quickly as she politely could, Beth told him she'd hold him to that lunch one day and strode off through the warehouse maze.

The raucous noise surrounding her seemed to mimic the clamor of her confused emotions. Once again, without even trying, he'd managed to thoroughly unsettle her. Even Lance hadn't run her through such a gamut of emotions. She'd felt sorry for him, angry on his behalf, saddened by her own secretive past. But most of all she had felt attracted to him. She couldn't deny it; it would be useless to try. She still tingled from seeing him smile. But before she'd even spoken to him today, she'd felt it; she'd been carried away by the mere sight of him.

A little over a week ago she'd thought him too thin and pale to qualify as handsome, but already the pallor was fading from his skin, replaced by the beginnings of a tan which would further enhance his dark good looks. His face was filling out, the chiseled features softening slightly, and his silky black hair was growing longer, erasing years from his appearance. A week ago he might

53

not have seemed handsome, but today she thought him almost too much so.

Slow down, Beth girl, she warned herself. *This isn't the sort of man for you to tangle with.* Being concerned about the employee was one thing, being concerned about the man was something else again. She hadn't come home from Minneapolis simply to jump from the frying pan into the fire. Resolving to put Kaler O'Connell out of her mind, she headed for her office.

But the image of his eyes still haunted her, ghostly gray and downturned in a sleepy sensuality she couldn't ignore.

Dee Branson intercepted her in the corridor, holding one palm up and one palm out. "Wait a minute, Beth. Do you have any change? I'd like to get a Coke, but I'm too lazy to go all the way back to my desk to get my purse."

"Sorry, but my purse is back at my desk too."

Dee's round face wrinkled in a comical mixture of disappointment and acceptance. "Some panhandler I'd make. Oh, well, I guess the exercise'll do me good," she drawled, patting her ample hips and grinning as she fell into step beside Beth. "On the other hand, it'll probably just stimulate my appetite. I'd better get enough change for a chocolate bar too."

"Sorry I couldn't help."

"That's okay," said Dee with a shrug. "I should've figured your purse would be locked up too. Isn't it a hassle?"

Beth threw her a puzzled glance. "What do you mean?"

"You know, locking our purses in our desk drawers. Don't you keep yours locked up?"

"No, I don't. Since when have you done that?" asked Beth, feeling that angry prickle crawl under her skin.

"Well, you know," Dee hedged. She wriggled uncom-

54

fortably under Beth's steady glare. "I mean, you've got to admit, it doesn't hurt to take precautions."

"Whose idea was this?" Beth demanded shrilly.

Dee gaped at the furious flush on Beth's face. "Well, um, you know—"

"No, I don't know. That's why I'm asking. Who told you to lock your purse up?"

"Leonard. He said he wouldn't leave them out anymore if he were us and really, it just made sense. . . ."

Beth didn't hear the words wither into nothingness. She had already wheeled and marched in the direction of the main office. All her earlier indignation returned, centralized on one person. Leonard was the one who hadn't wanted to give Kaler a chance. Leonard was the one hounding him now. Leonard was the one instilling nasty, vicious ideas in everyone else's head. Beth felt like strangling Leonard, but she contented herself with slamming into Nelda Evenson's office and insisting that something be done.

"Done about what, Beth?" asked Nelda with a flicker of concern for the glass rattling in her just-slammed door.

"Leonard!"

"Leonard?"

"Leonard Smolten," Beth clarified through clenched teeth. "Leonard Smolten and his snake-in-the-grass tactics!"

A slow smile started at the edges of Nelda's mouth and worked its way all the way up to her pale blue eyes. She ruffled the tight coils of her peppery hair with one hand and tapped a pencil with the other. Beth stood shaking with rage in front of her, unable to speak for fear of shocking her employer with language no one suspected she knew.

"I don't think," Nelda remarked at last, "that I've seen anything like this since that tornado flattened Elmer Jackson's barn back in fifty-six."

"Nelda, this isn't funny."

"Well, suppose you sit down and tell me what 'this' is so I can appreciate the seriousness of it."

Beth looked mutinous for a fraction of a second, then plopped into the armless chair beside Nelda's desk. She took a deep, steadying breath. "You backed my decision on hiring Kaler O'Connell, and I think you'll agree that we have to do what we can to help him adjust here. And that means putting a stop to Leonard's interference. He's undermining any chance Kaler has of gaining people's trust."

"Is that so?"

When Nelda used that tone, Beth felt about four years old. She bit her lip and went on more slowly. "Leonard's not only been watching everything Kaler does, which influences others to do the same, he's told Dee and the other women to lock up their purses. That sort of advice engenders distrust."

"And what exactly do you recommend we do to stop this insidious fiend?"

"Nelda! I'm serious."

Propping her elbows on her desk, Nelda interlocked her fingers and eyed Beth over the tops of them. All traces of jest went out of her mien. "I may not like this sort of thing any more than you do, Beth. In fact, I don't like it at all. But I can't fire Leonard for being Leonard any more than I would fire Kaler for being 'that wild O'Connell boy.' "

"I wasn't suggesting you fire Leonard—"

"No, but there's not much of anything else I could do. I can't tell him to quit being suspicious, he'd just think me a naive old fool."

A rueful smile touched Beth's lips. "He's as much as told me I'm a young one."

"If people wish to listen to Leonard and keep their valuables under lock and key, who are we to say they're wrong? If it makes them feel better, can we demand they don't do it? Beth, I think you should let time take care of these things."

"You think Kaler will be all right?" she asked, her voice irritatingly wavery.

"Kaler O'Connell," Nelda said firmly, "strikes me as a man perfectly capable of taking care of himself."

She didn't know if she believed that. He seemed so lost somehow, like a soul without a home; she ached just thinking about it. But she recognized the sense behind Nelda's words; she could see that her own interference wasn't any better than Leonard's. Silently vowing not to stick her nose into it anymore, she nodded at her employer and started to rise.

"Hold your horses. Stick around a minute. I've given you my opinion; now I'd like to have yours. What do you think of these designs? I met this young woman when I went to that crafts festival in the Ozarks. She works with stained glass, but it struck me that her designs could easily translate into needlepoint. Would you agree?"

And thoughts of Kaler were, for the time being, submerged.

She wasn't even thinking about him when she saw him. Standing beside her car, tugging the pink cotton of her blouse away from her sticky skin, she happened to glance out over the field beyond the lot. A lone figure was stretched out in the grass. She hung back momentarily, feeling uncertain about disturbing his solitude, then impulsively strode toward him.

As she neared, her gait slowed to a halting walk. His dark hair shone like raven's wings in the sunlight as he bent his head over a book. Disappointment nipped at Beth. He was reading; she shouldn't bother him. About to turn back, she halted when he glanced up and caught sight of her.

"I didn't mean to disturb you," she hurriedly explained.

The book was shut with a swift slap. He straightened. "You're not." That wasn't quite truthful. She always disturbed him, though it was as pleasurable as it was painful.

"I was about to go out for lunch when I saw you," she explained in a rush. "Would you like to come along?"

"Is this a subtle hint that I still owe you one?"

He sounded more relaxed than she'd ever heard him and her own tension drained away. Her voice took on a teasing lilt. "Are you questioning my intentions, sir?"

She was treated to that mellow chuckle of his. "No, ma'am. But I have to pass on the lunch. I'm fasting. I try to about once every ten days or so to clean out my system. Do you ever do it?"

"Are you kidding? I love to eat. I'd sooner go without sex than without food."

What on earth had possessed her to say *that?* To her relief, he merely laughed again. She couldn't know how difficult it was for him not to make some suggestive comeback. But that sort of light flirtation was impossible. His past was a barrier between them. He strove not to even think of it, but try as he might, he couldn't control the flood of sensations that threatened to drown him whenever she was near. For once he was grateful for the long years of practice at hiding his true feelings. At least he could keep her from seeing how affected he was.

"I'd be happy to feed you if you want," he said now.

Blond hair whisked as she shook her head. Her appetite forgotten, she sank to the ground beside him and carefully tucked her pink seersucker skirt around her thighs. "No, let's stay. I'm not really all that hungry and it's lovely out here. Do you come out here often?"

"Every day. I like to be out in the open. And the lounge reminds me too much of places I'd rather forget."

She plucked a fistful of grass, gently sifting the blades through her fingers. She scanned the plain black binding of the book he'd tossed aside. "What're you reading?"

"Nothing much," he hedged. Seeing the slight stiffening in her back, he realized that if he didn't wish to alienate her, he had to quit being so damn defensive. It was now or never; he'd reached a crossroad of sorts. He picked up the book and handed it to her. "It's called *The Hate Factory.*"

Their fingertips grazed as she took the book from his hand. Their eyes met, each mirroring a sexual shock neither wished to admit. They shared a hunger that had nothing to do with food.

Beth was the first to drag her gaze away. She fixed unseeing eyes on the book and flipped the pages silently, waiting for her heart to steady, her breath to return. When it had, she inquired, "What's it about?"

His smile was neither teasing nor sensual this time. It was rueful. "Prison."

The book seemed to weigh heavier in her hand. "Oh," she murmured, not knowing what else to say.

"It's about the uprising in New Mexico a few years back. Most prison books I've read were pure bull, but this one comes close to the truth."

"Why read it?" she asked pointblank. "I'd think you'd want to get away from all that, forget about it."

Only an innocent like Beth would think he could possibly forget. "I don't want to forget," he stated flatly. "I want to remember exactly where I've been . . . and where I'm going."

A gentle breeze capered through the grass, but it didn't cool the heat searing Beth's skin. She had to know; she had to hear it straight from him. Into the thudding silence she blurted out, "What happened, Kaler? What went wrong?"

He shrugged, smiled flippantly. "I got caught."

"Please, don't," she pleaded softly.

"You know what happened. Everybody does." Repressed emotion roughened his voice.

"I was only sixteen when you left. I never really knew all the details."

"My God, you must be the only ignorant soul in town." He shifted restlessly. He had known it would come to this. Sooner or later it always came back to this. His past oppressed his life. But if he were ever to come to an understanding with Beth, it couldn't be avoided. As much as he dreaded it, he had to try to explain. But what should he say? If he said too much, she might think he was making excuses, too little, and he might not convince her how much he regretted his past mistakes. What to say? How to begin?

He crossed his legs Indian-style and stared out over the flat horizon. Just grass and sky, nothing in between. As always, the view soothed him. And at last, he began at the beginning.

"I was what went wrong. My life seemed to go wrong from the beginning. My mother deserted us before I was even five. My old man was a drunk whose favorite pastime was beating me. While I was still small enough not to fight back, that is. You know, I was twenty-six before I had the courage to tell my father he'd never once said he loved me. He said, 'It's a bit late for that now, isn't it?' I said, 'I guess it is' and hung up. It was too late. He died four months later."

He didn't look at her, which was probably just as well. Beth would most likely have burst into tears and she knew instinctively how much that would upset him. She locked her grief inside, where her soul rocked with suffering for him.

"I grew up thinking I had to take on everyone in sight," he continued. "Take them before they took me. All I ever wanted was out. Out of Pasque, out of my kind

60

of life. But I was mired in it. I knew it was expected of me and I did my best to live up to it, directing all my energy to being *the* O'Connell to end all O'Connells. More and more I followed my father's footsteps, drinking and fighting and wasting my life. Of course, he thought it was only natural. In a way I think he even approved."

Kaler risked a glance her way. Her head was bent, her face veiled by a golden cascade of hair. He was almost relieved he couldn't see her reaction. He couldn't bear to see her shock, her distaste. Hoping with all his heart that she wouldn't hate him for what he'd done, he forced himself to continue.

"I'd had a ongoing feud with the owner of the hardware store. Old Cy was always egging me on, calling me a punk, daring me to prove to him that I was. Then one day, when I was with a pal of mine, he said some things about my parents I took exception to. We'd been drinking and when my pal suggested we teach the old bas— man to have a little more respect, I agreed readily."

The edge of the book bit into Beth's palm. She couldn't lessen her grip. She felt if she let go of the book, she'd let go of her control and throw herself against him in a burst of tears. "So you robbed him," she whispered in a voice hoarse and shaky.

Anger, fear, even a touch of self-pity, gnawed at him, and he burst out, "I was a nineteen-year-old kid with a chip on my shoulder and a grudge! I was drunk and angry, but even while I was in the act of robbing that store, I was regretting it. A thousand times I've wished I could go back and change it all. If I could, God knows I would. But I can't. I can't change the past."

"I know that!" cried Beth. She'd been afraid to speak, almost to breathe, but she could no longer remain silent. She'd hurt him and in hurting him she'd pained herself unbearably. "I'm sorry, I'm sorry. I didn't mean to stir up old wounds. What happened then doesn't matter."

"It does matter. It matters every time I call my parole officer, every time I see someone avoid me, every time I realize how much of my life I wasted. But if I can't change the past, I can change the man. And believe me, I've changed."

"I know you have," she said more calmly. "That's why I wanted to hear your side of it. What you did never seemed to match up with the man I know you are. I wanted to understand it. Thank you for explaining."

Joyous relief flooded his soul, lightening and lifting him. She didn't hate him; she didn't even think less of him. "You don't need to thank me. I wanted to explain. I wanted you to know that I'm trying to turn things around. I'm living up to my expectations, no one else's, and I expect myself to make good."

His voice trailed away like a cloud and his mouth crooked in a rueful smile. "It's so easy to go wrong and so damned difficult to set it all right again."

"How many men even try?" she asked in a soft whisper.

Kaler came abruptly to his feet. Once again she'd stirred up emotions he hadn't thought he still possessed. He felt wrung out and more than a little vulnerable. He hated to admit it, but he couldn't deny that his past mattered; it mattered too damn much. He spent every day of his life facing up to it; he couldn't believe she would be able to disregard it. His relief began to fade and was replaced by uncertainty. After she'd thought about it a bit, he felt sure she'd realize what a mistake it would be to get involved, however innocently, with him. And he didn't think he would be able to bear the hurt of her inevitable rejection.

He retreated behind a defensive aloofness, saying coolly, "I've bored you long enough. Besides, we've got to get back."

Beth unfolded her legs and rose. As she flicked bits of

grass from her skirt with one hand she held out his book with the other. He didn't take it. "You can borrow it if you like," he said.

Her brow puckered slightly. She felt torn. She felt as if she wanted to know everything there was to know about him. Yet she shied away from learning what kind of hell he'd lived through. "Thanks, but no," she said finally.

Already the rejection had begun. Kaler accepted it with uncharacteristic fatalism.

CHAPTER FIVE

June melted away in a heat wave that wrung out the community and worried the surrounding farmers. "It's gotta rain soon" was a continual refrain heard from the bank to the community center. By the Fourth of July worry was becoming resignation. It would be another bad year. News that Joe Schultz had gone under brought a nodding of heads and a round of speculation as to who would be the next to lose his farm. As July and the heat wave progressed, scarcely anyone remembered to be concerned over having that O'Connell back in town. Scarcely anyone, in fact, seemed to remember he was in town at all.

Kaler welcomed the quiet neglect. It was preferable to the mute animosity he'd first received and it bestowed the freedom that comes with anonymity. After years of constant crowds, of never having a moment to himself, he relished the solitude. Whenever he could, he walked the open prairie beyond town, enjoying the fragrant, clean air, talking to the wildflowers, reveling in the boundless view. He'd often sprawl in the grass, hands beneath his head, and gaze at the popcorn clouds floating across the vast blue sky. Eventually his eyes would drift closed and he'd remember the clinging buff skirt and how it had molded to her curves, wrapping against her legs as she moved. He'd picture the slit sliding apart and he'd imag-

64

ine rubbing his hand over the softness of her thigh. He'd imagine the pliant warmth of it filling his palm. His hand would slowly rise higher and higher and he'd be roused with imagining the touch and taste of Beth Rasmussen.

Kaler could feel himself getting worked up, just thinking about getting worked up. He cursed under his breath and tried not to think about it, about her. It was a waste of time to be losing himself in such fantasies. He'd made his decision, the only decision he could have made.

Other than a couple of brief, unavoidable conversations, Kaler had kept his distance from her. Whenever she came into the warehouse, which seemed to be less and less frequently these days, he'd found reasons to busy himself elsewhere. Though at first she'd tried to draw him out, reminding him of the lunch she was due and teasing him about his excuses, she eventually quit pressing him. He told himself he was glad she had, but that was not true and he knew it.

Loneliness was no stranger to him. He'd lived with it all his life. He knew, or thought he knew, how to live with the emptiness. But over these past couple of weeks the empty hours had become longer, the barren days bleaker. At times he could feel it eating away at him, corroding his strength to survive.

He jotted a notation in the shipping log and reminded himself he didn't need anyone else. He'd never had anyone else; he'd certainly never been able to rely on his parents. No, he had only himself and that was just fine. He liked being alone.

He glanced up, realizing that he was just that, alone. The warehouse had emptied out a half hour earlier; he'd stayed on to finish filling the log and had wasted his time daydreaming instead. Closing the log with a snap, he took it into Dutch's office, where he laid it on the desk. He switched off the lights, then made his way back through the darkened warehouse. His eyes adjusted easily and he walked quickly, his stride long and confident through the now-familiar aisles. As he neared the exit he quickened his step and rounded the last corner.

He smacked into the darkness, felt a jarring impact, heard a smothered exclamation, and saw a silhouette tumble backward. He shot out his arms, but grasped only air. Beth crashed into a pillar of cartons yet to be loaded onto the trucks. The cardboard shaft wobbled, then toppled. Boxes pitched in all directions, landing with thuds and thumps all around him. He heard her land with a resounding *thwack;* her cry of pain rang in his ears.

He knelt, his heart pounding wildly. "My God, are you hurt?"

She sat perfectly still, gawking at him through a cascade of golden hair, wishing one of the boxes had knocked her unconscious. She hated knowing she must look like an utter idiot, sprawled out, with her legs and arms splayed, her skirt bunched up around her thighs, and her hair tangled over her face.

"Are you hurt?" he repeated, his voice almost gruff. "Should I get a doctor?"

Pushing the hair out of her face with both hands, she offered a weak smile. "No, I'm fine. I mostly just had the breath knocked out of me."

"Are you sure?"

His obvious anxiety surprised her. After the way he'd steered clear of her recently, she'd figured he'd care more about the crushed boxes than about her. "Well, I think so," she said cautiously. "I probably bruised my dignity more than anything."

To prove her point, she tried to scramble to her feet. Pain shot up her right leg, and she teetered and sank like a setting sun beneath the toppled cartons.

He grabbed her, easing her backward tumble. "You *are* hurt," he said in an accusing tone.

A feeble smile wavered over her mouth. She nodded and pointed down at her right leg. "My ankle."

He followed the direction of her extended finger past the exposed thigh and shapely calf to the small turn of her ankle. He swallowed dryly. The hours he'd spent visualizing her leg. He assumed the most virtuous bedside manner he could manage and cupped her ankle in his hand. Though he probed gently, she still winced.

"You've definitely given it a bad wrench." God, she was slender, fragile, as delicate as china. She could have broken the bone so easily. Something within him constricted. "I'm sorry, my God, I'm sorry. But I never meant to run you down. You're the last person in the world I'd ever want to hurt."

An inner tingling dwarfed her physical aches. It seemed to radiate from where those long fingers circled her ankle, searing all the way through her skin. "Don't be silly," she said shakily. "It was as much my fault as yours. I wasn't looking where I was going."

The gnarl within his gut uncoiled; the strain of his muscles eased. He'd been blamed for mistakes all his life, yet the one time he'd willingly accept all the blame, she wouldn't let him. He looked at the pinch of pain upon her features and wished he could absorb all her hurt as easily as she absorbed his. "I think I'd better get a doctor," he said.

"There's no need for that. It's just a sprained ankle. I do it all the time. Usually I don't need anything this spectacular. I once sprained my ankle just walking across a room. Honest." She flashed a mouthful of gleaming white teeth at him.

"But we ought to do something," he persisted. "I can already see the swelling."

"I just need to soak it in ice water. Maybe you could round up some ice and after I've soaked it a bit and the swelling's down, I can drive on home."

Kaler scanned the shadowed room and knew it would be impossible. It was too dark, too deserted. If just one soul ever learned she'd stayed there alone with him, her reputation would be in shreds. *His* reputation would make sure of that. No one would ever believe the sprained ankle was anything but a cover. Old-fashioned as it seemed, he couldn't compromise her.

He removed his hand and said tonelessly, "It would be better if you went straight home."

Her ankle was throbbing more violently now and she'd begun to realize her bottom felt like a dented fender. He was giving her that remote look she hated and she decided she'd like nothing better than a good cry. In a voice laden with unshed tears, she mumbled, "I can't drive over three miles with a sprained ankle."

"We could call your parents," he suggested.

She wouldn't have thought it possible to feel so stung by rejection. After Lance, she'd thought she was immune to that sort of pain. But obviously she'd been wrong. Kaler didn't want her intruding in his life, not even for a few minutes, and it hurt. It shouldn't have hurt now at all; he'd made his feelings clear long before this. But it did hurt terribly. The welling tears spilled forth in a gigantic sob.

"Oh, God, don't cry," Kaler whispered, reaching for her.

She blindly thrust his hands away. "You don't need to bother about me," she gasped between sobs. "I'll take care of myself."

"Don't be a little fool," he said unevenly. "Stop crying and let me help you up."

With a defiantly loud sniff she allowed him to lift her to her feet. He steadied her as she gained her balance, his heart slamming in his chest when she leaned a hairbreadth away from him. He knew he should let her go and run to the nearest phone. But he lingered over the softness of her skin beneath his fingertips, over the faint hint of jasmine wafting from her silken hair. He savored the slight mist of her breath and the dewy moisture of her drying tears.

Nerves jumped in panic beneath the hands that clasped her arms. Her pulse leaped out of control. Her tears dried and she knew she should tell him to release her. But if she were honest enough to admit it, she'd have opted to have him hold her more tightly still. Beth, however, wasn't ready to admit this, not even to herself.

"I'll drive you home," said Kaler, after what seemed like an eternity.

She swiped a hand over her nose. "You don't have to do that. I can drive myself."

She might as well have saved her breath. As if she'd not raised the least objection, he put his arm around her waist and half-lifted her. Deciding might was right, she leaned against him, and together they hobbled unsteadily outside.

Her heart thumped more fiercely with each uneven step. The throbbing in her blood surpassed that of her injured ankle. She was scarcely aware of her ankle; she was scarcely aware of anything beyond the arm crossing her back, the hand resting on her hip, the solid musculature of the man beside her. He was all firm sinews and tanned skin. She luxuriated in his physical strength. Slanting more closely against his side, she told herself she was doing so only because she'd been knocked dizzy.

His senses filled to overflowing. Her profile dominated his vision; her hushed breathing resounded in his ears. He inhaled the sweet scent of her perfume and absorbed her soft warmth as she pressed against his side. Each sensation tantalized him, teasing his imagination. By the time they reached her car he was aching with desire.

He helped her into the passenger seat with something akin to relief. He walked slowly around to the driver's side, striving to focus his thoughts on something besides the painful excitement of wanting her. The sun hung low in the sky, blistering over the pavement, coating his skin with a damp heat. He felt burned all the way through.

He delayed a moment more, then got in. He had to strain to fit his knees beneath the steering wheel and she laughed a breathless, nervous little laugh. "The lever's on the side," she said.

After sliding the seat back, he sat immobile, staring at the dash and wondering if he even knew how to drive the damn thing. They said it was like riding a bike, you never forgot, but the heavy sinking in his stomach made him think they didn't know what the hell they were talking about.

She tapped his arm and he jerked away. "The keys," she explained, dangling a set above the gears. "It helps to use the keys."

He accepted them with a feeling of doom. He ought to get out while he still had a chance. It wasn't worth the risk; nothing could be worth it.

"Is anything wrong?" she asked

He glanced at her. She appeared puzzled, a bit wary. He could take anything but having her fear him. "Not really," he said, trying to sound casual. "It's just that I haven't driven in . . . a long time."

"Oh," she said, then licked her lips. "Kaler, you really don't have to—"

"Don't worry, I'll get you home in one piece," he interrupted. Hoping he could make good on his word, he wiped his palms down the legs of his jeans, then turned the ignition. As he drove out of the lot, he thanked the Lord it was an automatic.

Creative Crafts sat at the outer edge of Pasque, the field beyond the parking lot merging with the surrounding prairie. Beth's great-grandparents had pioneered this land, homesteading in a sod house on the site where her

70

family farm now stood. She issued directions, then subsided into reflective silence. It would have been easier, she mused, to bump along in a covered wagon, pursued by savages, than to sit calmly beside Kaler, trying to ignore the heat sticking to her skin and the fever rising in her blood.

Kaler was grateful she didn't seem to expect him to make small talk. Under the circumstances, he wouldn't have known what to say to her. But even without words, even with the unfamiliar driving to distract him, he remained tensely conscious of her. Each time she shifted even slightly, his body warmed in response.

Eight years without a woman. It was little wonder that her mere proximity roused him so readily. Yet he was certain that if he'd spent the last eight years in a sheikh's harem, he'd still react as strongly to Beth. She was a uniquely beautiful person. . . .

He glanced at her. Framed by silken tumbles of blond hair, her profile had a classic old-world aura. To him she looked fragile and feminine and unbearably desirable. He riveted his gaze to the road.

No longer tucked within the unsettling circle of his arm, Beth regained enough of her senses to wonder what on earth had come over her. What would her parents say when she rode up with Kaler O'Connell? She might as well come home with John Dillinger. Why hadn't she sensibly phoned them when he first suggested it?

Why hadn't she indeed? Such questions were better left unanswered.

The tar-patched road crawled beneath the wheels with such agonizing slowness, Beth was certain she could have limped home more quickly. Surely this drive had never before taken so long, nor had her car ever been driven so carefully. She surreptitiously checked and was surprised to find he was keeping to the speed limit. She couldn't believe they could be moving at that speed and still be

71

taking so long to get home. Each minute confined with him, locked in this silence with her recriminating questions, seemed neverending.

And then she saw the old county road sign that marked the last stretch to home and felt she barely had any time left with him at all. She rushed into speech, not even realizing that she'd been planning her apology all along. "Kaler, I'm sorry about all this, about disrupting your evening and—"

"You didn't. Believe me, there was nothing to disrupt." Not this or any other evening.

"I shouldn't have bothered you," she persisted. "I really do thank you for going out of your way like this for me."

He couldn't believe his ears. Didn't she realize that he'd have done far more for her, carried her home on his back if necessary? He'd never felt such concern for anyone in his life as he had when he'd seen her face whiten with pain, and now she was actually apologizing to him. It affected him in a myriad of ways, ways he couldn't define.

"Don't worry about it," he said in an offhanded way that had nothing to do with what he was feeling.

She pointed toward a dirt road on the left. "Here. This is it."

As he turned onto the road he could see a leafy maple standing on either side at the end of it. A hedge ringed a neatly mowed yard. Columbines bent in the wind, their pink and white petals dusting the grass before a white frame house with red shutters. Kaler thought it looked like something out of a fairy tale.

He parked in back as she instructed, then came around to help her out. Her heartbeat accelerated as she again accepted his support. With his arm slung around her, Beth staggered from the drive to the back steps. Even the distraction of his touch couldn't suppress her discomfort.

The pain was worse now, shooting through her with each tiny jolt.

Kaler took one look at her wan face and didn't hesitate. He swung her up in his arms and lithely mounted the steps. She didn't protest; she didn't want to. She felt secure, comforted. Her only regret was that there were so few steps. At the top she pulled open the screen door and he shouldered through. It snapped shut behind them as they entered a large country-style kitchen.

"Beth? Is that you?" called an unseen woman. "Hurry up, we just sat down."

"Which way?" asked Kaler, whispering.

"Follow your nose," she whispered back.

He strode through the kitchen, watching their wavering reflections pass from shining appliance to shining appliance. My God, it was clean. Sparkling clean and deliciously aromatic. His nose led him to the left of two doors, where he paused. Knowing he should set her down, he hated the thought of letting her go. He'd probably never get another chance to hold her. He decided to make the most of this one. He pushed open the door and entered the dining room with Beth firmly clasped in his arms.

There was an absolutely still moment in which shock rippled down the table, from her mother to Ted to Jenny to Dale to her father. The second wave of reaction was more varied, including her parents' concern, her sister's intense interest, and her brothers' antagonism. Beth watched their changing expressions and felt her pleasure in Kaler's arms fade. She wiggled within his grasp, indicating she wanted to be set down, but he simply tightened his hold and announced, "Your daughter's twisted her ankle; it looks like it could be a bad sprain."

There was a touch of aggression in the statement. Beth looked at him in sharp surprise. He'd never used that tone in her presence, not even tonight when he'd been so

73

determined to bring her home. But the surprise she felt was nothing compared to that of her family's; she could see it darkening the room and decided the moment called for a quick explanation.

"It was one of my stupid accidents," she said hurriedly. "I fell in the warehouse and if Kaler hadn't been there to drive me home, I don't know what I would have done. My ankle's already the size of a tennis ball."

Her mother rose with a series of brisk instructions. "Jenny, get towels and the Ace bandage. Dale, bring me the plastic tub from in the basement. Ted, the footstool's up in my sewing room."

Chairs rasped, voices clashed, steps rapped over hardwood as the younger Rasmussens jumped obediently to her bidding. Emma briefly inspected Beth's ankle, told her to get her shoes off, then whisked into the kitchen. Kaler felt rather as if he'd walked into the eye of a hurricane. Frank Rasmussen recognized the look and actually laughed, startling him.

"It takes a bit of getting used to, Emma's whirlwind efficiency. Even after more than thirty years together, I still find the wind knocked out of me when she's like that."

"Yes, sir," said Kaler, feeling at a real loss. He'd expected hostility, demands to unhand his daughter, at the very best a reserved thanks. He would have known how to handle any of those, but this left him dumfounded. He watched warily as the older man came to his feet and moved to the side of the table.

"Unless you're of a mind to hold on to her forever," said Frank dryly as he pulled out a chair, "I'd suggest you put Beth down here."

"Yes, sir," he repeated. He'd rather have held on to her, but he set Beth on the chair, then backed into a shadowed corner. Her father fluffed her hair, then bent to remove her shoes. She began relating the accident in amusing detail and the two laughed together. The loving intimacy made Kaler feel like an intruder. Beginning to wish he could simply vanish into thin air, he edged toward the door.

It flew open and Emma swept in, followed by a stony-faced Dale, and within minutes Beth's foot was soaking in a round tub of ice water. She yipped at the frigidity and both brothers claimed she deserved it for being such a klutz. Jenny returned with the towel and bandage, as well as a plump pillow. She'd hardly set them on the sideboard when her mother sent her to fetch another place setting for Mr. O'Connell.

Hearing this, Kaler started. He couldn't possibly intrude any further. Already he'd stayed too long. He didn't belong in a home like this, and he knew better than to wish he did. "That's not necessary, Mrs. Rasmussen," he said flatly.

"But of course you're staying to dine."

"I don't think I—"

"Have you eaten?" she asked.

"No," he admitted.

"Then you will eat with us. It's the least we can do for your kindness to Beth. Sit down, please."

She sounded like a schoolmarm. He could almost picture her short, graying hair rolled into a tight topknot and her petite figure decked out in a severe dress. Her oval face had the same old-fashioned charm he'd seen in Beth's; she looked a lot like her daughter, small and feminine, but Emma had an inexorable way of speaking that he didn't think Beth would ever cultivate. Perhaps being the mother of a large, boisterous brood had made it necessary for her to sound as if she meant whatever she said. But just the same, he couldn't quite accept that she meant this. She couldn't really mean for him to sit at her table, share her food. After all, he was an O'Connell.

Frank cleared his throat. "The house rule is that Emma's never wrong at dinnertime. So I suggest you sit yourself down while you're still able to do so." He winked broadly at Beth, who shook her head at him.

She saw that perhaps this was all too much for Kaler. For the uninitiated, meeting the Rasmussen ensemble could be like meeting an eighteen wheeler head-on. But she longed for him to stay. She gently tapped the chair beside her and said, "Someone will have to drive you back to town, Kaler. If you don't stay, that'll be two missed dinners instead of one."

He still hesitated, wanting very much to stay but believing strongly that he shouldn't. "I can walk—"

"Walk! Are you kidding?" shrieked Jenny as she skipped in, her hands filled with a plate and silverware. She whistled as she laid the dishes on the spot between her sister's and her own. "That's crazy. It's over three miles to Pasque."

He glanced at the brothers. Neither had spoken, but they didn't need to. It was perfectly apparent they'd prefer having the flu in for dinner.

"Our meal is getting cold, Mr. O'Connell," Emma pointed out.

He gave in. He'd wanted to, anyway, but now he could do so in good conscience. The brothers could go hang. He sat down and bent his head while Frank intoned grace. This must be the way it is in real families, he thought. The way it might have been in his family if his mother hadn't run off, if his father hadn't been a drunk, if he'd been loved and secure. If, if, if.

Buttery baked squash, beef casserole, boiled new potatoes, and powdery biscuits attracted his attention. He realized he was famished and dug in with relish. For a few minutes the sound of a meal in progress dominated the room, but then the Rasmussens got down to their nightly discussions. They spoke of general things—the weather, the economy, the withering crops; they spoke of specific

76

things—the next day's chores, Marilyn's pregnancy, Ted's approaching departure for college. The loving warmth enwrapped Kaler. He luxuriated in the comfort of it. Emotions began churning within him, tender emotions he'd thought long dead, emotions that somehow centered on Beth.

He permitted himself a covert look at her. She contributed less to the conversation than the others; she was more subdued, which struck Kaler as a distinct contrast with how she outshone the others in looks. Her hair, her features, even her smile were definitely brighter. Perhaps her smile seemed brighter because she offered it more sparingly, making it more special. Jenny grinned constantly; she seemed never to stop moving, her long ash-brown hair flying about her shoulders as she twisted this way and that on her chair. Beth sat far more still; she seemed to him to be an oasis of tranquility in the midst of this volatile family.

She unexpectedly looked his way. The clear blue understanding of her gaze melted into the gray yearning of his. A moment passed, then another. Kaler became aware of the growing silence around them and averted his eyes to his plate.

"I think," Beth announced, "my foot has gone numb. I can't feel a thing, not even the water."

"Just keep that foot where it is," ordered her mother. "As soon as we're done here we'll wrap it, then you'll keep off it as much as possible."

"Kaler could help her do that," suggested Jenny. Her wide grin became an enormous one. "Can't you just see it? Kaler carrying her from the chair to the couch, from the couch to bed?"

Silverware stilled for a fraction of a second. Jenny didn't seem to realize her faux pas, though the expert way in which she avoided Beth's murderous eye con-

77

vinced her older sister she not only realized it, she enjoyed it.

"Anyway," the teenager babbled on, turning directly to Kaler, "when you came in carrying Beth in your arms, I thought you looked just like Clark Gable in *Gone With the Wind*. You know, when Rhett sweeps Scarlett up the stairs. God, how exciting! But even without the stairs you looked terribly romantic," she finished generously.

"Jenny," Beth growled. But she wasn't really angry; one look at Kaler and she couldn't be. A half smile played over his lips, and he appeared more at ease. Silently she sent her sister a kiss of gratitude.

"So what happened anyway?" demanded the irrepressible Jenny.

"I knocked Beth down," said Kaler, then smiled into Jenny's blue eyes.

"Actually I ran into him," Beth clarified. "I deserve a sprained ankle for not looking where I was going."

Jenny bounced on her chair. "Saaay, Beth, with that bad ankle of yours, I guess I'll just have to drive you to work tomorrow, huh?"

"If you're thinking of driving my car all over kingdom come, you can just forget it."

"How else will you get to work? You can't drive yourself. You wouldn't have gotten home tonight if Kaler hadn't driven you." She flashed a confident grin at Kaler, as if to say, *I got her on that one.*

"Speaking of that," drawled Dale, and Kaler tensed. He knew the note of trouble when he heard it. He knew the look, too, and Dale definitely wore it. Dale leaned back in his chair, narrowly scrutinizing him, as if he'd been waiting for his chance and was about to seize it. "Speaking of that," he repeated, "it's occurred to me that I haven't seen you driving around before. At least, not since you got back from prison."

78

Reddening, Beth thought fleetingly of giving Dale a swift kick, sprained ankle and all.

"That's probably because I haven't been driving around," said Kaler in a measured tone.

"Do you have a license?" Dale asked sharply.

"No."

An uncomfortable hush settled over them all. Frank and Emma exchanged a look, Jenny squirmed, Ted shifted slightly away from his brother. Beth sat as still as a stone, not stirring by so much as a breath.

Well, all dreams come to an end, thought Kaler. He'd felt all night as if he'd been in a dream, the sort of fantasy he hadn't allowed himself to indulge in since he was a child. He'd leave them to decide whether they wanted to call the authorities and report that O'Connell had finally violated his parole, just like they'd all known he would. He started to push back his chair.

"More cobbler, Mr. O'Connell?" asked Emma, reaching for the cherry dessert.

He checked, looking from the cobbler to her in questioning surprise. She pushed the dessert toward him. He slowly shook his head. "No, thank you."

"If he doesn't want it, I'll take it," Jenny offered.

"What you'll take," corrected her mother, "is a stack of dishes to the kitchen."

While his wife and daughter began clearing the table, Frank pulled a pack of cigarettes from the pocket of his green plaid shirt and tapped one out. "Now tell me, Kaler, have you ever done any farming?" he inquired on a conversational note.

Kaler's gaze shot to him. Frank's weathered face wrinkled in a kindly way, but Kaler didn't lower his guard. "No, sir," he replied charily, "but I've always thought I might like to."

"It's a different operation from when I first started out. Cigarette? No? Ah, well, you're smart not to. I got the

79

habit when I was younger than Ted there and never've been able to get rid of it. So you'd like to try farming?"

"Yes," he said. To work with the land was his idea of paradise.

"It's a hard life nowadays. Used to be a simple struggle with the elements. Today farming's mechanized, computerized, a complex corporate game. The little guys are being forced out."

"But, Dad, don't you think the small farmers are still the backbone of the business?" asked Ted.

"Maybe today, but not tomorrow." Frank then launched into an explanation prolonged by spirited interjections from his youngest son.

With a brusque "Excuse me" Dale stamped from the room. His exit seemed to go unnoticed by everyone except Kaler. He stared at the vacated chair, almost wishing Dale had not gone. He knew how to deal with that type of animosity, it was the others' kindness that unsettled him. A hand touched his knee. He cast a startled eye toward Beth. She smiled a soft, sweet smile that made his heart turn over.

"Don't worry about Dale," she said. "He'll get over it."

He wasn't worried about Dale, not in the least. It was this upheaval within himself that had him worried. What he said was, "Maybe it's time I got on my way."

But he didn't go. He stayed to carry Beth out to the den, lowering her gently into an overstuffed chair more comfortable than chic. He stayed to watch as Emma dried and wrapped her daughter's ankle, and to watch Beth in the glow of muted lamplight. He stayed to listen to Frank's dry observations on the local political campaigns. Most of all, he stayed to pretend, for a short while longer, he was a part of it all, to imagine he belonged.

It passed all too quickly. Though he tried to hold it back, the time spun away. It seemed a matter of mere seconds before Frank rose, stretched, declared they ought to be going while he was still awake enough to drive.

Reluctantly Kaler came to his feet. "Thank you, Mrs. Rasmussen," he said with stiff formality. "I don't know when I've had such a delicious meal, nor such a pleasant evening."

He wasn't exactly being truthful. He did know. He'd never had food that tasted so good; he'd never had an evening so imbued with a welcoming warmth.

"Nonsense," said Emma in her brisk way. "It's we who thank you—for bringing Beth home. It couldn't have been an easy decision for you to make."

"He should've let me limp home," Beth put in. "But he's too much of a gentleman."

Their eyes met and Kaler felt a surge of desire unlike anything he'd ever known. The heat blazed from his loins to the center of his being. Some gentleman, he thought with self-derision, and harshly reminded himself that such desires could never be fulfilled.

Suddenly glad to be leaving, he bid her a restrained good-night and strode out.

CHAPTER SIX

Emma Rasmussen believed in big breakfasts. Her large oak table fairly groaned beneath the weight of platters stacked with pancakes, plates heaped with eggs, and pitchers brimming with fresh farm milk. Hand on hip, she stood beside her chair and surveyed the array.

"Well," she said as she did every morning, "are you going to let it all get cold?"

As if on cue, hands shot out to pass platters and plates around the table while chattering voices harmonized with clashing silverware.

Only Beth remained silent. She'd wakened in a listless mood, an apathy spawned by the depression she'd taken with her to bed the night before. It had been so unexpected, that abrupt withdrawal of his as he said goodnight; her joy in the evening had instantly crumbled.

Up to then she'd felt a blossoming happiness. Her heart had swelled with love for her parents, for their acceptance of Kaler. She had not even known how very much it meant to her until Dale had made it so clear that he, for one, did not accept Kaler. But even that had not dampened her spirit. It had taken Kaler to do that. One long look at her and he'd withdrawn. She'd seen it in his eyes, she'd heard it in his voice, and she'd ached with the grieving pain of loss.

Her reaction stunned her, then depressed her. She

didn't understand her sense of loss, but she did understand that she didn't want to feel such things, not on his account, not on any man's account. One time through that particular emotional wringer had been more than enough for her.

She pushed a forkful of eggs around her plate, not really caring about eggs or anything else. She dimly realized her mother was speaking to her. "What?" she asked dully.

"I asked how your ankle was this morning," said Emma, giving her a sharp look. "Do you think you should stop by Dr. Drake's and have it x-rayed?"

"No. I'm sure nothing's broken. It's not even that much of a sprain, just a twist really."

"Still, you'll probably need to be driven to work today," Jenny said hopefully.

"Sorry to disappoint you, little sister, but I think I'm capable of driving myself."

"You probably were last night," Dale muttered.

Beth set her fork down and stared across the table at her brother. "What do you mean by that?"

He expertly speared a pancake from the platter centered on the table and plopped it onto his plate before replying. "I'm just wondering how bad your ankle was in the first place. Did you really need an escort home? Or were you using one of the oldest female tricks in the book?"

"That, Dale Matthew, is a rotten thing to say. But even if I had been using such a trick—which my swollen ankle more than proved I was not—what concern is it of yours?"

"You just happen to be my sister," he answered. He set the syrup bottle down with a whack. "And I'm very naturally concerned when my sister comes home in the arms of a known criminal."

She sucked in a hissing breath, then released it with

slow, careful precision. "That's what he was," she clipped, "not what he is."

"Come on, Beth, how naive can you get? He is what he is, what he always has been."

"Don't you believe in giving someone a chance? Don't you think people can change?"

"Change? Are you kidding? He violated his parole just last night."

"He was helping me out, at risk to himself."

"He was breaking the law," he said. "Again," he added with pointed emphasis.

"Well, *I* think it's incredibly romantic," piped up Jenny. She struck a pose, aiming an imaginary gun. "Beth could team up with him, you know, like *Bonnie and Clyde.*"

"That's just what I'm talking about," said Dale, his square jaw thrusting forward in disgust.

"Oh, for the love of—" Beth swept up her fork and stabbed at her eggs, then dropped it with a ringing clap. "All he did was bring me home!"

"Probably to see what we had worth taking."

A heated flush crept up her neck to her cheeks. She thought of a dozen retorts, but bit them back. It would be futile to go on arguing. Dale was too certain he was right to be swayed by anything she said. Perhaps, given time, he'd reassess his judgment of Kaler.

"I can't believe," Dale suddenly flared, sweeping his angry gaze around the table, "that you're all so complacent about this. Do you *want* Beth to get involved with a convict?"

Silence crackled through the room. Each of them, even Jenny, sat immobile, paralyzed by the grip of tension.

"What we want, son," their father finally stated, "is to enjoy our breakfast in peace."

An awkward shuffling of feet preceded the mute resumption of the meal. Beth ate nothing at all. Shoving her plate away, she mumbled her excuses and limped into the kitchen. She was angrily slapping mayonnaise onto bread when Emma came in behind her.

"Do you think there might have been a mistake at the hospital?" asked Emma.

Beth dropped lettuce and sliced beef onto the bread. She looked at her mother sidelong. "What?"

"Do you think perhaps I was given the wrong child? Dale can be so bullheaded on occasion—he simply can't be mine. It must have been the hospital's error."

"I don't feel like being humored, Mother."

"No? What do you feel like?"

"I feel like knocking some sense into Dale."

"Now, isn't that odd? I've the distinct impression that he feels precisely like doing the same to you."

The knife clattered to the floor. Beth swore under her breath and reached for a clean one. As she did, Emma put a hand over her daughter's, stilling the restless agitation. "For what it's worth, Beth, I don't think you need sense knocked into you. But I do think you should take care."

She met her mother's unfaltering gaze. Tolerance shone in the blue eyes so like her own, but concern dimmed the brightness. Beth's temper cooled and she sought to soothe Emma's fears. "You needn't worry, Mom. Dale's blown this all out of proportion, that's all."

"I'll always worry about my children—"

"That's what mothers are for," Beth finished. A smile played over her mouth. She'd heard that one so many times, it was probably engraved in her heart. "Okay, Mom, worry all you want. Who am I to stop you? But believe me, there's no need to waste your energy."

Emma wagged a finger at her, then headed back to the dining room. At the door she turned and added, "Oh, and Beth, why don't you take him that extra piece of cobbler with his lunch?"

She sailed out before Beth could close her dropped jaw. After staring blankly at the door for a few seconds she grinned and blew a kiss to the air. Then she reached for the cobbler and two more slices of bread.

Holding two sack lunches, Beth waited in the lounge. She knew his routine almost better than he did. He'd stop by the machines, get a sandwich and a soda, and slip outside. But not today. Not if she could help it. Where, after all, was it written that they couldn't be friends?

The murmuring that drifted through the room would have told her he'd entered even if the jangling of her nerves had not.

Bracing herself, she welcomed him with a wide smile. The low hum around her deepened. She paid no attention to it. Her attention was riveted on Kaler; he eclipsed everything and everyone else. He always had. In the old days, if she'd thought about it at all, Beth would have assumed it was due to his cocky stride, his bold stance. He'd had a way of looking as if he owned whatever piece of property he happened to be standing on. He didn't look cocky now. Yet his effect was precisely the same.

As usual, he had a book in one hand. He swept the other through his glossy black hair, which, longer now, fell in soft layers. Beth's mouth went dry. She beckoned him. He wavered, then slowly approached.

How often had he fantasized about a woman with a welcoming smile? How painfully had he yearned for it? Kaler tried to tell himself she smiled at everyone, she was generous with her smiles, she didn't know what it meant to him. But a thrill shot through him nonetheless.

A dozen things to say flew through her mind, but she'd had time to remember all the occasions he'd rebuffed her over the past few weeks and she remained silent. Would he reject her again? Had last night changed anything?

"Hello," she managed at last.

86

"Hi. How's the ankle?"

She stuck out her leg and wiggled it. The beige bandage was barely visible beneath the hem of her navy slacks. "Much better. It didn't even really bother me driving in this morning."

He clicked his tongue against his teeth. "Poor Jenny," he said solemnly. "I hope she survived the disappointment."

Feeling as buoyant as a balloon, Beth laughed lightly. "She was utterly crushed, but revived remarkably when Scotty Weston drove up in his pickup."

They shared a knowing grin. It was new to Kaler, this sharing of a simple, silly memory. But a rising tension pierced his pleasure. He glanced around. Anticipation gripped the room. As little as he wanted to, he knew he had to put an end to this sweet interlude. And still he lingered.

She cleared her throat. "Thank you again for taking me home last night. But you really shouldn't have taken the risk—"

"Forget it. I was happy to do it." He gave her one of those conversation-ending nods and made to move away.

"I brought lunch for you," she said quickly. She held up a paper bag. "Mom even sent some cherry cobbler as a special treat. If you don't help me out, I'm going to have to eat two lunches all by myself."

She waited for him to say something, but he just stood and stared at her. "Are you fasting again?" she asked.

He stared, not really believing the entreaty he saw in her lovely eyes. He longed to touch the curve of her lips, to feel the smile he was seeing, and know the reality of it. But her smile faded into a puzzled frown. She tipped her head and the silken gold of her hair whisked softly. He stared and he hungered, but not for the lunch.

"It's roast beef," she tried again, dangling the bag in front of his nose.

87

He came to his senses. A swift survey told him everyone had heard, that everyone still watched avidly. "Thank you," he said stiffly, "but—"

"Don't you dare try to decline my mother's cobbler," she interrupted. She knew by his stiff response just what he'd seen in that quick appraisal and all her indignant hackles were raised. She sounded amazingly like Emma at her schoolmarm best. "Now, if you'd be so kind as to get us something to drink, I'd like a cola."

Without waiting to see if he accepted her imperative invitation, Beth began unpacking the sandwiches. By the time she removed the foil-wrapped cobbler, it was obvious she'd left little doubt in anyone's mind that this lunch had been prearranged. Throughout the lounge the buzz of speculation took on the drone of certainty.

Kaler thought she'd gone mad. He quietly said as much when he returned with the sodas. She answered with a pat to the metal chair beside hers. He didn't move.

"Don't you care that they're all talking about you?"

"No," she said simply. "Do you?"

Kaler knew when to give in, especially when he wanted to anyway. If she didn't care what they thought, he certainly wasn't going to try to convince her otherwise. He sat down, set his book aside, and picked up his sandwich.

"Glad to see you've got such good sense." She pushed a piece of cobbler his way. "If you don't eat this, you'll receive one of my mom's infamous tongue-lashings."

"Lord, spare me that," he said in mock horror. "I've known wardens who could take lessons from your mother."

She sputtered, choking back her laughter. "You shouldn't joke about a girl's mother."

He found himself smiling again. It was remarkably easy to smile around her. He felt lightheaded, giddy, high on nothing at all. "I don't think," he drawled, "that I'd call your mother a joke. I happen to admire her a great deal."

It was on the tip of her tongue to say something ridiculous like, *You're gorgeous when you smile like that,* but she sensibly swallowed the inanities and said breezily, "Oh, you're right. My mom's no joke."

His smile wavered, then faded. He looked down at the scratches crisscrossing the tabletop. "Last night," he said haltingly, "meeting them . . . I enjoyed myself very much." He'd never be able to express how much.

"I'm glad, Kaler, really glad. We enjoyed having you. Maybe you could come again sometime."

"But not too soon," he said without thinking. He felt her stiffen and sprang into an explanation. "I didn't mean that the way it sounded. To tell you the truth, I'm not used to being social yet. I live alone . . . it tires me out, trying to talk to people."

Happiness danced through her. He'd been tired when he left last night, that was all. She grinned happily. "That's not at all unusual with us. The Rasmussen clan can be a bit like an avalanche, I know, smashing the poor unsuspecting into oblivion, but taken in small doses, we're rumored to be tolerable."

"More than tolerable, from my viewpoint," he said. "I kept thinking last night that I'd walked into the middle of a Norman Rockwell painting come to life."

There was a tinge of yearning in his tone. Beth looked away, picking a bit of fat from the edge of her roast beef. "You really shouldn't have driven me home, Kaler. It wasn't worth the risk."

He shifted uncomfortably. "I told you, forget it. It's over with, no damage done."

"But what could have happened? What if we'd been stopped?"

"We weren't, so why talk about it?"

89

"But if we had been, Kaler, what then? I think I've a right to know."

He could see she wasn't going to let it go. Sighing in exasperation, he said gruffly, "I'd probably have gone back to prison to finish my sentence. My p.o.—parole officer—is a real by-the-book hack."

She hung her head. Her hair fell forward, veiling her face. "You shouldn't have taken the chance," she whispered. "Not on my account."

He thought his heart would simply burst. Never, not once in his life, could he remember anyone caring what he did or what happened to him. Never had anyone sounded so concerned for him. He longed to sweep her into his arms, to hold her as he had last night, to kiss her as he had all night in his dreams.

Forcing an easygoing note into his voice, he agreed. "You're right. Next time you hurt your ankle, I'll leave you alone. If it's broken, I won't come near you."

She peered around the tumble of her hair. "I wasn't talking about me. Just my car."

"It's a deal," he said, and she smiled so sweetly he had difficulty pretending to eat his sandwich.

"What're you reading this time?" she asked, licking a stray crumb from her lip.

He watched her tongue dart around the fullness of her mouth and swallowed dryly, trying to collect his scattered thoughts. All he could think of was how much he'd like to dart his tongue over her lips. He finally tore his gaze away and managed to reply. *Uncreated Freedom.* It was written by a guy I knew in the joint. A priest, actually. It's a speculation on how far the human imagination could extend in matters of faith."

Her nose wrinkled. She eyed the book suspiciously. "It sounds too deep for me. Deadly deep."

"It's pretty dry," he admitted with a chuckle.

"I wonder about some of the stuff you read. Keep it up

and you're going to forget how to think like the rest of us simple folk. Maybe I should assign you to a strict diet of P. G. Wodehouse or something."

She began to clear the table, neatly folding one paper bag and putting it inside the other, stacking the two cups together, and crumpling the plastic wrap into tight balls. He imagined what it would be like to have her doing such things for him, the way Emma had done for Frank, to know the delight of her teasing smile and warm kindness all the time, to share with her the quiet times, the private times. Such sweet dreams were bitterly tormenting and utterly useless. He pushed them from his mind.

"Spoken like a true schoolmarm," he told her.

"You can't take the marm out of a teacher," she laughed.

"You're a teacher?" He was truly surprised. There was so much about her that he did not know, had no right to know.

Her laughter waned. She slid her gaze away from his. "I was."

The small evasion told him a great deal. He wanted desperately to ask her about it, to say, *Tell me, share your sorrow with me.* He wanted to ease and comfort her. But Kaler was the last person on earth to probe into another's painful memories. "Well, that explains why I sometimes felt like you were giving me the big exam" was all he said.

It was what he didn't say, didn't ask, that spurred her to explain. "I taught in Minneapolis. Second grade. I thought the young ones would be more manageable. Boy, was I ever wrong."

"So you didn't like teaching."

The statement held a question, one Beth longed more than anything to ignore. But she couldn't. He'd opened up to her probings. Now it was her turn to keep the slender thread of communication between them from snapping. She traced aimless little patterns across the ta-

91

ble with her fingertip. "No, I liked teaching well enough. It was . . . Minneapolis . . . that didn't agree with me."

Kaler had learned to spot a lie; in prison his life had sometimes depended on it. But in a world without a moment of privacy he'd also learned to respect the sanctum of another's privacy. "I can understand that. You must have missed your family, gotten homesick."

"I did miss them, I missed them all. But they were the main reason I left in the first place."

He didn't look as if he believed her. He didn't. Given a family like the Rasmussens, given the love and the warmth, the caring and the sharing, he'd have stayed put for eternity. They said you couldn't miss what you'd never had, but they didn't know what they were talking about. He'd never had the loving support of a family like the Rasmussens and he'd missed it like hell.

Watching the disbelief cross his face, she laughed softly. "I didn't mean to imply that I didn't love them or that I wasn't happy at home."

"Then what did you mean, Beth? It's incomprehensible to me that you'd want to get away from your family."

The husky way he breathed her name prompted her to reveal more than she'd intended. "You remember how you told me all you'd ever wanted was out? Well, I wanted out too. I needed to be on my own, to be alone, to stand out on my own. I don't suppose you can imagine what it's like, since you're an only child, but sometimes seven just seemed to be about six too many. I always got lost in the crowd."

He couldn't imagine losing her in a crowd of thousands.

"With three older and three younger, sometimes I just felt like a shadow lost amid the bright lights. I felt invisible. I longed to stand out in some way from the rest of them. It always seemed to me that I didn't have anything that made me special."

He thought everything about her was special.

Holding up her hand, she began counting off on slim fingers. "I lacked the favored distinction of being first like Charlie or last like Jenny. I wasn't as pretty as Marilyn or as witty as Rita. Dale's more outgoing and Ted's more intelligent. I was just the quiet one."

He knew she was the desirable one. She was the most desirable woman he'd ever known.

"Beth," he said softly, "you're more sensitive, more caring. You're a very generous and warm person. You needn't ever feel less than anyone else."

She became absorbed in a scrap of foil, fluting the edges between her fingers. She couldn't meet his gaze for fear she'd blurt out the awful truth; she couldn't bear to have him think poorly of her, as she knew he would.

At length, she went on. "When I was a teenager my need for attention flared up in little ways, what Mom calls my ornery streak. I remember one year Dad got involved in a local county election and everyone practically lived at the candidate's headquarters, making signs, handing out literature, running errands. But I went to work for the rival candidate." She sent a self-deprecating smile his way. "We won too. But I didn't really care about the election. I was just being rebellious."

Kaler eyed her for a long moment. Rebellious, he could tell her about being rebellious. Finally he shook his head and sighed heavily. "I am deeply shocked," he said solemnly. "They should've hauled you in and thrown the book at you."

She balled up the foil and threw it at him. He caught it and gave her another of his beguiling smiles as he popped it into the stacked cups. "I suppose," she said with mock hauteur, "it all must sound pretty stupid to you—"

93

"No," he interrupted, suddenly serious. "Not stupid, Beth. Blessed."

"What?" She blinked at him in stupefaction.

"Blessed. It sounded to me as if you were blessed." His voice was husky with emotion. He couldn't make a fool of himself in front of her. He pushed back his chair and jerked to his feet. He stayed a moment more to thank her.

And in that moment, she did feel blessed.

CHAPTER SEVEN

"May I give you a friendly word of advice?" Leonard didn't wait for her assent, but closed her office door and camped his lanky form on the corner of her desk. "I hope you'll take this in the spirit it's given—"

"Oh, I will," Beth interrupted dryly.

"And I assure you with all sincerity that I say this with the utmost good will," he went on, completely unaffected by her discouraging tone. "I'm concerned, not only as a member of this company for a fellow employee, but I am concerned about you as a friend. You can't know how worried I've been—"

Well, at least she agreed with something he said. She couldn't know. To be honest, she didn't want to know. Clearing her throat, she said, "Leonard—"

"How worried we've all been," he continued. "I've taken it upon myself to express to you what so many of us feel."

She rolled her eyes, but leaned back in her chair and prepared to listen. It was obvious the only way she'd get rid of him was to let him have his say, then politely show him the door.

"As a supervisor myself, I can understand your . . . commitment to an employee you've personally hired. A rash act," he digressed, "I still firmly believe to be a mistake you'll one day come to rue."

"He's been doing very well. Dutch is pleased with his work."

"For now."

"For over six weeks now," she corrected him.

He pressed his glasses up the thin bridge of his nose and regarded her through the thick lenses. "Well, that's neither here nor there. What I wished to say is that you've apparently allowed your tender-hearted charity" —he made the term sound like a social disease—"to obscure your good sense. You've carried things too far."

Even while telling herself she didn't have to defend herself, she protested. "I can't see the harm in a few lunches, Leonard."

"You have had lunch with him every day this week. Every day this week, Beth."

"Guilty as charged," she said flippantly.

Leonard was not amused. He frowned heavily at her. "Already you're being unduly influenced."

Her fingers itched to hurl her stone paperweight at him. From some unbelievable source, however, she managed to retrieve a shred of patience and leave the stone in place. With cold politeness, she inquired, "Are you through yet?"

"As young and trusting as you are, I merely wished to warn you against permitting yourself to mistake your sympathetic concern for this . . . employee . . . to be anything more than what it is."

"Thank you, Leonard, for the warning," she said through her teeth. "I assure you I'll give it all the consideration it deserves."

At last he removed himself from her desk. He ran a hand over the brown wisps of his hair and heaved a sigh. "I don't suppose you'll listen to me," he said with gloomy certainty, "but I had to speak up. Everyone who works with you, everyone who knows you, shares my concern.

An innocent young woman like you involving herself with a man like—"

"Yes, well, I appreciate all your concern," Beth cut in briskly. She stood and walked to the door. She opened it and held it wide. "Do, please, convey my appreciation to everyone else."

Shaking his head, Leonard left. Beth slammed the door, wishing she'd let herself throw the paperweight after all. Sarcasm was too good for him. Storming back to her desk, she flung herself into her chair and inhaled deeply. After the fifth big breath, she calmed a bit. A second later and she began to giggle. Solicitous advice from Leonard Smolten, of all people. It was a wonder he hadn't started in on the dangers of the birds and the bees!

Her laughter pealed as she pictured Leonard lecturing her on the birds and the bees and the hazards of mixing the two. She could see him pausing to wipe steam from his Coke-bottle glasses and nearly choked. Wait until she told Kaler about it!

She stopped laughing. No, this was one thing she wouldn't be telling Kaler. Although she'd come to realize he had a strong sense of humor, she didn't think he would find Leonard's dire warnings amusing. And they weren't.

She had placed herself on the outside; she had made herself a target for the collective censure of her community. She had done so from the moment she packed that first lunch for him. And with every day that passed, every lunch she and Kaler shared, she slipped further and further away from the circle of acceptance.

But Beth didn't care. What she gained in those few hours with Kaler more than offset anything she may have lost. Bit by bit, a friendship was blossoming, a special kind of friendship.

Though they shied away from the type of deeply personal revelations that had marked their first discussions,

97

every other topic was fair game, from politics to religion. They found they agreed more often than not and congratulated each other on having such good sense. As she came to know more of him, Beth became increasingly impatient to know even more. She felt rather as if she were on a treasure hunt, digging up the most unexpected prizes.

She learned he was intelligent, extremely well-read in philosophy, poetry, the classics. Contrary to her earlier fear that he couldn't think like simple folk, he was equally comfortable discussing Agatha Christie or the latest Michener novel. He explained wryly, "I had a lot of time for reading."

She learned he had old-fashioned values. He believed strongly in the bonds of marriage and family. He had strict views on fidelity and familial responsibility that had momentarily surprised her. Later, she'd realized it didn't surprise her at all. Given his background, given his lack of family support, she understood just how important family would be to him.

Sometimes they were serious, like the day she asked him about the friends he'd made in prison. He shrugged. "There weren't any."

"But surely, in all those years—"

"You can't get attached in prison. It's a transient world. The faces are always changing. And once somebody's gone, they're gone out of your life. Prisoners aren't permitted to communicate with one another. So you learn not to get attached."

She bent her head, trying to hide the sadness this made her feel, the sadness of all those years he had to suffer without someone to lean on. But she wasn't able to hide anything from Kaler. He chucked her under the chin and drawled lightly, "Does this mean you're sorry to hear I'm unattached?"

"Utterly devastated," she'd managed to say with a laugh. But she wasn't sorry about it at all.

Sometimes they were not so serious, like the day he tried to explain what he called his misspent youth. "What I needed was an attitude adjustment," he said. He tapped his skull and grinned rakishly. "The lobotomy did the trick."

Their ringing laughter produced a round of silence among their coworkers, but Beth didn't care. So long as she could hear his laughter, she didn't care. She had remembered him as a young man filled with a love of life and laughter. His enjoyment in life had been suppressed, submerged beneath a defensive detachment. Gradually his true personality was reemerging, and Beth was fascinated by the transformation.

Thinking of transformations, Beth shook herself out of her reveries and onto her feet. She should have left fifteen minutes ago. Her extension club had arranged for an aerobics class and she had to change as well as drive to the Presbyterian church in all of ten minutes. Using the company's ladies' room to change, she rapidly slipped out of her cream silk blouse and khaki slacks and into a teal terrycloth jumpsuit with crimson piping on the cuffed shorts and sleeves. She was knotting the laces of her worn sneakers when Lisa Ingram entered.

"Oh. Hi," Lisa said, stopping on the threshold. Her long dark ponytail whisked as she looked over her shoulder, apparently giving thought to backing out.

"Hi. You're here late." Beth hoped she sounded casual.

Lisa came all the way in. "We were backlogged on orders. I stayed to get them into the computer. Overtime, of course."

"Of course." Straightening, Beth gathered her things together. "Well, 'bye."

"About you and that O'Connell," Lisa said abruptly.

Beth froze in the doorframe.

"I don't care what Eddie says, I think he's okay," Lisa declared in a rush. "He works hard and doesn't cause any trouble. Besides, he's a real good-looker and if he ever set eyes on me the way he does on you, I wouldn't care what he'd done either."

Beth managed not to smile. "Thanks," she said, and left. The encounter buoyed her; as they had after she'd hired him, people would gradually come to accept him. She whistled cheerily as she drove the few short blocks to the church and carried the tune with her down to the basement meeting room. There she was greeted with conversations dwindling into dead silence and grazing glances of chilling brevity. It was a curt reminder that acceptance wouldn't come easily.

"Hello," she called as merrily as she could.

Martha Hanson sniffed audibly, but a few actually returned the salutation. After an uncomfortable lapse in which Beth had time to note the sign on a Sunday-school bulletin board that read DO UNTO OTHERS, Harriet Trowbridge crossed to pinch a handful of the teal terrycloth and exclaim loudly, "Why, Beth, if this isn't the cutest darned thing I've seen in an age! Did you make it yourself?"

Though she half-suspected Harriet's action stemmed more from a desire to ruffle Martha's feathers than to soothe her own, Beth nonetheless gave her a grateful smile. "I'd be happy to lend you the pattern."

"You know there's no sense in that, I'm all thumbs." She tugged on Beth's arm, pulling her toward the women clustered beside an old upright piano. "Just take a look at this outfit Beth made. Isn't it something?"

A small silence replied. Eyes again skated quickly past her. Shoulders half-turned as Patsy Lackey, Ruth Doyle, and Gail Walkingstick formed their own tight knot that distinctly excluded her. Anne Young clicked her teeth, though whether over the outfit or the person in it was uncertain. With a sinking heart Beth understood she wasn't going to win any popularity contest here tonight.

"Say, Beth, what are you doing here?" asked Sally Green. She sat on the piano bench, her hands folded atop her belly. "I wouldn't think you'd be able to do anything so strenuous with your sore ankle."

Feeling the need for support anyway, Beth sank down beside her. "The ankle's fine, all right and tidy. But what about you? You're the last person I expected to see at this meeting. Unless you've heard that aerobics induces labor or something?"

"No such luck. Nine days overdue already and going for a tenth." Her ready smile faltered. She lifted a hand to push her dark hair back from her brow. "I just came to watch, but maybe you're on to something. Maybe it'll be inspiration."

Beth laughed. "For your sake, I hope so. It must be rough being pregnant in this heat."

"That's putting it mildly," Sally groaned. She gave Beth an arch look. "Just wait till you find some nice young man; see what you have to look forward to?"

The innocent statement seemed to have another message. She examined Sally's well-rounded face and decided her suspicions were groundless. She was becoming paranoid. Sally didn't mean anything.

Just the same, depression crept in on Beth. Finding a nice young man wasn't as easy as it sounded. She knew; she'd tried. She really wondered if she ever would. Both Marilyn and Rita had been married long before they'd reached her age. Candace had been only twenty-one when Charlie married her. Even all her high school chums were old marrieds, most of them with young children already. Beth was well past what Pasque considered the normal marriageable age. In another era she'd be called a spinster.

The instructor bounced in, flashing pearly teeth and

shapely muscles, and Beth got up in a dejected way to join in the exercises. "My name's Wendy," bubbled the young instructor, "and we're going to feel sooo good tonight! Right?"

"That's what you think, lady," muttered Candace as she stepped into line beside Beth. "Lord, I don't know why I let the rest of you talk me into this."

"Because you're secretly into S and M?" suggested Beth.

"All right, girls, let's hop to it!" Wendy exhorted as she flipped on the reel-to-reel she'd set up earlier.

To the energetic beat of a tape recording more than amply loud, they kicked, skipped, and jounced, running out of steam long before Wendy did. Beth decided if she heard Wendy gurgle one more time that they were going to firm those muscles and fight that flab, she'd run screaming from the building. Just when she thought she might run, Wendy clapped her hands and announced a break. Moaning in unison, the small group collapsed.

"Remember my friend Alexis, Alexis Pavelka?" huffed Candace.

Beth dragged air into her aching lungs and assented.

"Her brother-in-law's been accepted into veterinary school."

"That's nice."

"He's going to be in town for a few weeks, staying out on the Pavelkas' farm."

Involuntarily Beth's stance took on a defensive rigidity. "What's this all about, Candy? Are you trying to fix me up?"

"Not if you're not interested," she replied, unperturbed. "But if you should decide you might be, Jay will be around for a couple of weeks."

"Thanks, but no thanks," responded Beth as pleasantly as she could. It was quite a feat, as she wasn't feeling very pleasant. "I have notoriously bad luck with blind dates."

102

"That could be taken care of," Candace began, but Wendy sprang to Beth's rescue, crying, "We're all raring to get back to work, right? So let's go!"

By the second break Beth sensed a conspiracy in the making. Having happened, said Irene Bauer, to overhear Candace mention Jay Sturgess, she couldn't help relating that she'd met Jay at the Pavelkas' last Christmas. "Such a nice young man," she said, and Harriet echoed, "A nice young man." The phrase caught Beth's ear. She darted a look at Sally, who was deep in discussion with Patsy and Gail. Perhaps she wasn't paranoid after all.

Within five minutes she was certain she wasn't. Gail came first, stepping into place beside Beth and complaining wearily that she was pooped. "Another round and I'll have to be carried home," she wailed, then quickly added, "But you must be really worn out—after working all day at the plant and all."

"It's not any more tiring than housework, Gail."

"No, not physically, but you've got to deal with so many problems. Employee relations and all."

Patsy chimed in, "You've got a point, Gail. Why, I wouldn't want Beth's job for anything, having to handle all the responsibilities she does." She gave Beth a look brimming with sympathetic understanding. "You made a tough decision when you took on O'Connell; it must take a lot out of you to stand by it."

Beth let it pass, flinging herself into the bobbing and bouncing with new vigor. The pattern was beginning to take shape. Divert her with a "nice young man," then stress the not-so-niceness of the one threatening her, sweetened by a heavy dose of understanding. Her first reaction was sheer anger. At least Leonard had had the courage to tell her outright, even if he did dress it up as "friendly advice."

But, as always, her wrath was fleeting. Leonard hadn't been exaggerating when he'd said everyone was concerned. They were. She could see it in their eyes, in the way each of them found it so difficult to speak to her. It touched her, this comprehensive caring about what happened to her. Even as she resented the interference, Beth was affected by the solicitude.

Hot, sweaty, and confused, Beth welcomed the end of the evening. She was one of the first to leave, making her good-nights hurriedly, and escaping up the stairs. She wasn't quite fast enough however. Candace reached her side before she reached the top.

"Hold on a minute, Beth. I'd like a word with you."

Thoroughly tired, feeling as if she'd been plowed under a ton of conflicting emotions, she wanted nothing less than to hear another word about men, nice or otherwise. "Some other time, Candy. I'm really bushed."

Candace wasn't so easily dissuaded. "I won't take long. I just want to ask you to think about what you're doing."

She blew out a long, bitter breath. Hadn't she already heard this lecture? But she didn't evade the point. "A few lunches together. What's so awful about that? All we've done is talk."

"It's what those talks will lead to that worries us."

"You expect us to make love on the tabletops?" she asked cuttingly.

A flash of hurt clouded Candy's expression. "For your own good," she said, "just don't forget what he is."

"He doesn't have leprosy; his past isn't contagious!" Beth exploded in exasperation.

"We don't care about his past, Beth, can't you see that? We don't care about him at all. It's you we care about, you and your future." Candace clasped her sister-in-law's shoulders and gently shook her. "We love you and we don't want to see you hurt. We don't ever again want to see you looking like the whipped puppy you were when you came back from Minneapolis. So, please, think about those innocent little lunches and just what exactly you're getting into. Okay?"

Her heart knocked painfully against her rib cage. It seemed to take a lifetime for the word to come to her lips. But inevitably, it did. "Okay."

On the heels of her promise, she broke free of Candy's grasp and bolted up the last of the stairs.

She kept to her word. She thought about it. In fact, she thought of little else. With careful deliberation she assessed the value of the hints and warnings she'd received. She easily dismissed the common fears that Kaler was either a dangerous man or a villainous one. Despite what he'd done nearly nine years ago, Kaler was industrious, reliable, determined to reshape his life. She knew no one would believe it, but he was far more conservative than she, even on legal issues. No, she wasn't worried about Kaler's past, nor even about his possible recidivism.

She was worried about Kaler the man. The sensitive, intelligent, gentle man who could make her heart sing with his laughter and sigh with his quietude.

More than anything else Candace had said, it had been the remark about the whipped puppy that caused Beth to seriously ponder just what she might be getting herself into. As much as it galled her to admit it, she had returned from Minneapolis with her head hung and her tail between her legs. She'd been broken emotionally—at the time, she thought irreparably—but time truly does heal all wounds, and as she mended she'd clung to the certain resolution that she'd never again allow herself to be so hurt.

In the past few weeks that resolution had been endangered. Even in such a short time she'd revealed far more of herself to Kaler than she ever had to Lance. She'd made herself vulnerable to Kaler as she'd never done before, and all because Kaler was the one thing Lance had never been—her friend. And she treasured his friendship.

If friendship were all she felt for Kaler, she'd defy the whole town, the whole world if necessary, to preserve it. If friendship were all, she wouldn't give a fingersnap for anyone's opinion.

But unable to lie to herself, Beth admitted it wasn't all. She felt more, far more, for him. She'd been attracted to him from the first, from the day he'd walked into her office—no, even before that, from the moment she'd seen him walking down Main Street on the day he had arrived. Her heart pumping wildly, she hadn't been able to take her eyes off him. She had wondered even then what it would be like to touch the man behind the austere mask.

The more she came to know him, the more she wanted to know how he would feel beneath her caress, how he would taste upon her lips, how he would look in unrestrained passion. She often recalled the night she'd hurt her ankle, the warmth of his arms encircling her, the way his breath had misted her hair, and she would ache with longing for more. Each time he touched her, each brief grazing of fingertips or light brush of his arm, deepened her hunger to know what comfort, what passion, what joy lay within his embrace, within the gentle persuasion of his kiss.

More often, she saw an answering need within his darkening gaze, and with it she knew they were moving slowly, inexorably, irrevocably, beyond friendship.

For all that she was willing to be Kaler's friend, Beth wasn't ready to risk anything deeper. Her emotional scars were still painfully visible, too much so. Maybe later on she could take another chance on love, but not now, not yet. She had to back away while she still could, with her heart whole.

Her decision seemed preordained. By the time she en-

106

tered the lounge the next day, Beth felt as if this ending had been destined from the beginning. She had dressed for the occasion, wearing her most severe suit, a dull navy pinstripe that didn't really become her but gave her a protective aura of reserve. She wished she could as easily have donned a shield for her heart.

Kaler waited for her at what had become their table. Unlike the cautious restraint that had marked his first greetings of her, he met her with an open cordiality marked by one of his charmingly lopsided smiles. She couldn't bear to confront the allure of it; she dropped her gaze to the floor. As he always did, he stood and pulled a chair out for her.

Gathering all her courage, she delivered her rehearsed speech. "I'm sorry, I can't stay for lunch today. I've got a meeting to attend."

His smile slowly melted away. Disappointment flooded him. These lunches had become the highlight of his day, his life. But he managed a credible nonchalance. "Ah, well, tomorrow then."

"I'm sorry, I can't tomorrow either," she said stoically.

He took in the suit, the dispassionate demeanor, and his heart began to thud sickeningly. Dear God, no, not this, anything but this. He'd been so careful, so damned careful not to expect more. But he was totally unprepared to receive less. He couldn't bear it. He couldn't believe it; he wouldn't believe it.

"Maybe next week," he tried.

"Maybe," she agreed.

But they both knew the word had no meaning.

CHAPTER EIGHT

Dirt smudged her knees and sweat dampened her back. Her hair was pulled back and untidily restrained by a white plastic clip. The denim of her shorts was faded, the edges ragged with fraying threads, and the blue of her sleeveless blouse had bleached to a faint gray. All in all, she looked like a ragamuffin. Yet Kaler thought Beth had never looked lovelier.

He watched her from a distance, from behind a large maple while she yanked weeds from the garden. He watched and suffered the stirring torment of desire. His whole being ached with desire. He'd thought he wouldn't want her so much, not now, not after the pain he'd endured. He'd thought he'd deadened every possible emotion he could conceivably feel for her. But he'd been wrong. He wanted her more than ever before. He throbbed with the wanting. He wanted to touch her, to glide his hands over her curves, to press himself against her softness, to ease his aching within her. In all his life he'd never wanted a woman the way he wanted Beth.

It went beyond wanting. He needed her. He needed her gentleness, her kindness, her sweet humor. It made him feel sick, this wanting and needing. He couldn't have her. He could never have her. He hadn't even been able to keep her as a friend. She had come to her senses.

And with a single "maybe" she'd crushed his spirit as

eight long years of prison had never been able to do, as a lifetime without affection or acceptance had never been able to.

He didn't question why Beth had brought about the abrupt end to their lunches, why she'd severed their growing friendship. He had no doubt why. She had finally realized what everyone else already knew, that he wasn't the sort of man she should be encouraging, however innocently. He had to acknowledge that on his part it had never been so innocent. He'd wanted her friendship, it was true, but even more he'd hungered for her as a man craves a woman. He'd filled every fantasy with her image and with every fantasy his desire had grown. In some way he must have revealed his true feelings and frightened her away.

She stretched, arching her back and tilting her head, and his heart thumped violently. He forced himself to look elsewhere. A hanging basket of bright red blossoms swayed above the back porch. He considered slipping silently away, but pride kept him from leaving. He'd come with a purpose and could not leave before he'd accomplished what he had to do.

Careful of the package he held, he edged his hands down the sides of his jeans and stepped forward.

Even before she heard his footsteps, Beth stood still, a trowel in her hand. With prickling certainty she felt his approach. She gulped in a breath and slowly pivoted on her heels.

"Hello, Beth," he said.

"Hello, Kaler." She shielded her eyes with a hand and squinted up at him. He stood stiffly, his face closed, his gaze remote. Her heart gave a queer little lurch. She lowered her hand and though her legs were unexpectedly weak, came to her feet. They faced each other in an awkward silence.

109

"I never expected to see you this far out of town," she said finally, sounding stilted.

"You needn't be worried, I walked. I am allowed to walk," he remarked incisively.

She flushed, dropped her gaze to the ground. He silently swore. There was no sense trying to deny it. He had hoped for something else. He'd hoped for his own confident charm and her sweet smiles; he'd longed for a warm reception, not this wooden restraint. It was obvious she'd sooner receive heat stroke than him. He couldn't deny his biting disappointment. Kaler had wished for a miracle, but he should have known better. A childhood of wishing had brought him nothing but a manhood of emptiness.

Aimlessly kicking a clod of dirt with her toe, Beth chided herself. How could she sound so unwelcoming to him? How could she, when her heart was leaping with the joy of seeing him? Even if she didn't want to get involved with him, she could at least be cordial. Simple courtesy demanded it. The clod disintegrated into fragments and she returned her attention to him.

"Well, I'm glad you stopped by to say hello. It seems I never get a chance to see you at work anymore."

He didn't know which was worse, her lifeless reserve or her artificial congeniality. He regretted coming. It had all been for a stupid, prideful gesture—and an even more imbecilic hope. He decided to save them both any further embarrassment and leave. "It's hard when we're both so busy. But anyway, I should get on my way."

But she caught sight of the package in his hand. "What's that?" she asked, pointing, and he heartily cursed himself for bringing it, for coming here, for putting himself through all this pain. She was still staring at the package. He had no choice but to give it to her.

"It's for you," he said flatly, thrusting it at her. "You

110

never let me repay you for all the lunches you brought me. I thought this would clear the debt."

She took it with trembling hands. The wrapping on the rectangular box was a heavy cream vellum decorated with bright purple pansies. So old-fashioned, like him. Her mouth softened into a gratified smile. Kaler couldn't bear seeing her smile. He focused on the drive, thinking about the long, empty walk ahead of him.

"Oh, Kaler, you didn't have to do this. I adore Gibran."

He looked at her. She was smiling directly at him now, her face alight with pleasure, her fingers curled around the slim spine of *The Prophet*. When he thought of the hours he'd spent trying to decide which to buy. . . .

"I just saw it," he said, "and thought it would repay you."

She busied herself with folding the wrap into a neat square. The gift had touched her deeply. It went to the core of her being. She was grateful for far more than the book. She was glad, so glad just to see him again. She gripped the book tightly. "You didn't owe me for those lunches," she said.

"In any event, we're even now, so I guess I'll just—"

"You'll come in for a beer to cool you off," she interrupted with her best imitation of Emma. Simple courtesy be hanged. He was here and she wanted him to stay. She saw his hesitation and added persuasively, "Or lemonade if you don't like beer."

Thinking nothing could cool him off around her, and knowing he should leave, Kaler found himself saying, "As soon as I couldn't have it, beer was one of the things I missed most."

"Then come on," Beth ordered. They walked to the back porch and up the steps. She paused beneath the basket of begonias. He reached over her shoulder to pull the screen door open and her pulse raced as memory sparked. They'd come this way before, but then she'd been in his arms, snuggled against his heart, the warmth and strength of him thrilling her as even the mere memory did now. She knew a wish that he would remember too.

He did. His body pulsated with remembering. He could almost feel the bittersweet pleasure of her delicate curves held captive in his arms. The memory excited him and he strove to forget.

Inside, the big, bright kitchen was as clean and shiny as he'd remembered it, and he filled with new longing. He wished he'd left when he'd had the chance. What the hell had prompted him to accept her invitation? What had prompted her to issue it?

Beth fanned her face with her hands and blew straggling wisps of hair off her brow. His handsome features were darkened by a sadness it wounded her to see. More than anything else, she longed to see his smile, hear his husky laughter. She wanted to see the life return to his eyes. She could not let him leave looking like this.

"I'm glad you showed up," she said. "Not just because of the book, but because it's too hot to be working today. I'm grateful for the excuse to give up battling with the weeds. They were winning anyway."

Though she gave him an opportunity to speak, he said nothing. She raised her arms behind her head and unclipped her hair. It rippled free and she shook it loosely about her shoulders. She took her time about retwisting her hair and clipping it into place. Every moment was agonizingly delightful to Kaler. Just being near her, inhaling her scent, watching the fluid beauty of her motions, listening to each breath she drew, pleasured him. But it was a painful pleasure, knowing it was the last time for him to be with her like this. He couldn't allow himself to hope for more. Hope so often led to disappointment.

"I'd offer to drive you back," she finally said, "but I

112

insanely let Jenny talk me out of my car for the afternoon."

"That's all right. I don't mind walking. It's my main form of entertainment and exercise."

"Still, it's a long trek, both directions." She paused. "You could wait until Jenny gets home, then I could drive you back to town. That is, if you don't have anything else you need to do."

The hope he'd been trying to suppress would no longer be restrained. Hope surged through his entire being. Maybe, just maybe, he was being given a second chance to gain her friendship.

"There's nothing else," he said. "And to tell the truth, I'd be grateful for a lift home."

She presented a sunny grin. "Great. Do you like apples?"

Not waiting for his reply, she dug two golden delicious apples out of a basket arrangement on the counter and dropped them into a small plastic bag. She added two cans, one of beer, one of cola, then tied the top into a knot. "Ready?" she asked, her voice lightly merry.

He wanted to say, *For you, any day,* but all he said was, "Sure."

Beth led him outside, across the drive, and past the half-weeded garden. Along the way she thanked him again for the book, and before he could object she explained how much it meant to her. "I really do love Kahlil Gibran. I wasn't just saying that. So much of his philosophy aligns with my own. You know, like 'make not a bond of love,'" she quoted at random.

He stared straight ahead at the barn and sheds and at the fields beyond. The intermingling of barnyard odors filled him with the sweet smell of freedom. "I also agree with that one. I won't be kept in bonds of any kind; I've promised myself no more captivity."

She could feel the fluttering of the pulse in her throat.

113

She'd felt deliciously quivery ever since he arrived, but now she felt dangerously so. While she wondered at the precise meaning of his statement, she reacted to the obvious message in it. She debated within herself, then murmured, "You were in prison a long time, an awfully long time."

He sighed. Back to this; it always came back to this. He couldn't escape the invisible bars of his past. He skimmed his gaze over her profile. Had this been behind their rift? If it were, he couldn't risk not answering her unspoken question. "Yes," he said slowly, "I was."

"Longer than usual?"

"I never made it easy on myself," he told her directly. "Not from the beginning. I got an unusually stiff sentence for my unwillingness to aid the judicial process."

The quizzical look she gave him touched him, yet irritated him too. God, to be so unbelievably innocent! If it were any other woman, he'd be dead certain it was an act. But with Beth he had no doubt it wasn't. And it irritated him because he believed her innocence set them irrevocably apart.

A brief smile curved his lips as he translated for her. "I refused to rat on my accomplice. Cy Aldrich didn't know him and I wouldn't cooperate by fingering him. The tougher they got with me, the tougher I got with them."

They passed the barnyard and fenced hog pens to follow a narrow path through unmown grass. Cottonwoods hemmed one side of the path and they were squeezed together. She moved with hushed delicacy, her body whispering close to his. Trying not to notice either her body or his reaction to it, he continued. "I saw myself as some sort of noble loner, withstanding whatever punishment they threw my way. But I was just a scared and lonely kid acting like the tough I imagined myself to be."

A lump rose in Beth's throat. She jerked to a stop. As he halted beside her, she whispered, "I'm sorry."

"Don't be," he said quickly, sharply. Then he repeated more gently, "Don't be. It's all over and done with, long ago. And you shouldn't waste your sympathy on someone who was as thickheadedly stubborn as I was. I'm solely to blame for keeping myself behind bars."

"You caused trouble?"

Without thinking, he reached out to stroke away her frown. His fingertip touched the edge of her mouth, and as he felt her breath warming his skin, he caught himself and snatched back his hand. His every nerve jumped with the longing and aching to touch her. But he couldn't risk again scaring away the one friend he had. The only friend who'd ever meant anything to him.

Beth only barely stopped herself from begging him to go ahead and touch her. She wanted him to touch her. She wanted him to caress and to stroke and to love her. Her body fairly thrummed with the wanting.

Another second of throbbing tension and she would have broken the silence with her plea. But Kaler spoke first. "No, it wasn't that. I wasn't a troublemaker. I just didn't work within the system. I didn't play the game their way. I told you I'm not much for games."

"What do you mean? I don't understand," she said unsteadily.

"The first couple of years I was stupid. I spent my time loafing around, acting tough. Then I began to wise up. I took the yard job and began making use of my time. There's an old con saying: Do the time, don't let the time do you. It just took me a while to figure that one out."

"But why didn't you get paroled then? Didn't they see you were making an effort?"

"My uncooperative record hurt me," he explained. "Then, too, I never did any of the things the parole board looks for. I studied on my own, but that didn't matter to them. Schooling is one of the things they consider proof of rehabilitation, and I never took any classes."

He glanced down at her. Her fragile face was filled with concern. Knowing it was for him erased all the pain of remembering. He stripped a leaf from a tree and tapped her nose with it. "Now, if they'd had teachers like you, I'd have been the first one in class every day."

The leaf tickled. She blew it away. He laughed.

Did he have any idea, any idea at all, how sexy that smile of his was? Did he know what it was doing to her pulse, her heartbeat?

She wheeled around before she could give in to the need to wrap herself in his arms. They walked in wordless companionship, enjoying the sun and the faint breeze, the sounds of shrilling locusts and rustling grass. The bright sunlight spun white-gold threads through her hair, and Kaler longed to twine his fingers within the silky weaving.

At length, the path opened onto an expansive, stubbled field pocked with huge haystacks and dimpled with squat hay bales. Flinging a saucy smile up at him, Beth darted ahead, her figure lithe and lovely as she ran. He followed, catching up with her long before she stopped beside a stack almost precisely centered in the field.

"This one's my favorite," she said, as if that explained everything. She plopped the bag of apples and cans in his hands, then turned and dug in a toehold. Grabbing a handful of the haystack, which was more actually a tightly packed square of straw, she began hoisting herself up. "Coming?" she challenged.

By the time he got to the top she was sitting with her legs spread-eagled before her, vigorously rubbing her hands over them. "You'd think I'd have more sense than to climb up here wearing shorts, wouldn't you?" she asked. "Look what I've done to my legs—a mass of scratches."

He'd have been more than happy to rub them for her, to kiss each slight mark along the tanned calves, but he somehow resisted the urge to do so. Instead, he camped down beside her, opened the bag, and tossed her an apple. He drew out one for himself, as well as both cans and they simultaneously crunched into the fruit.

The sky held a mixture of blues, from near gray to vivid robin's egg, and was nearly cloudless, with just the merest wraith of a white smudge floating occasionally by. A breeze gentled the air and birds glided away with it. From their vantage point on top of the stack the prairie seemed to stretch into infinity toward the west, miles and miles with only an intermittent tree to interrupt the horizon. To the east, a bulbous water tower rose above the distant buildings that marked the town.

Eating her apple, Beth could only wonder how she managed to get anything down a throat so constricted. Her nerves seemed magnetized by his every movement, crackling each time he drew a breath. She felt more alive than she had in days, yet at the same time was oddly more at peace.

Gazing at the view, Kaler endured the discomfort and joy of being near her. He sweetly tortured himself with visions of pressing her down into the straw, kissing her senseless with all the pent-up need he felt, and caressing her into submission. He nearly groaned aloud. The frustration was enough to try a saint, much less a sinner like himself. Calling upon every fiber of strength he possessed, he forced the tantalizing images from his mind.

When she finished the apple, Beth placed the core into the plastic bag and wiped her fingers on her shorts. Drawing her knees up to her chin, she wreathed her arms about her legs and lay her cheek on her crossed arms.

He lay on his back with his hands pillowing his head and his knees drawn upward. He basked in the warmth of the sun and the contentment of being with her.

"Kaler," she murmured drowsily.

"Ummm?"

117

"Why did you come back here? You've no family left here. Why didn't you start fresh somewhere else?"

"You know, you missed your calling in life," he drawled. "You ask questions like a prosecutor."

Her head shot up. She intercepted his teasing smile and relaxed. "I just wondered. You might have had a better chance somewhere else, where people didn't know you and didn't care who your parents were."

Years of secreting his private thoughts, withholding his gentler feelings, of never letting on, made it difficult at first; it seemed to him that the machinery governing his finer emotions had rusted from disuse. But he wanted to share with her as he'd never done with anyone else and, eventually, he cranked the machine and opened up more fully than he had ever done.

"It was partly O'Connell bullheadedness. I never could do something easily if there was a harder way." He flashed a smile that held a rueful hint of pain and sat up.

Facing west, he looked out over the prairie. He inhaled the wonder of its beauty. A sense of tranquility soothed him. He spoke quietly, unhurriedly.

"Family or not, this was my home. All those years I kept dreaming of the wind running through the grasses, of unbroken miles of prairie. I never wanted to be hemmed in by anything again in my life, not by concrete, not by skyscrapers, not even by mountainsides. I longed for the vast serenity of the prairie."

"So many people make fun of the flatlands," she said. "I've always wondered how they could fail to see how lovely they really are, how peaceful."

"And you, like I, came back to it."

"Yes," she murmured, "yes, I did."

It wasn't fair to expect disclosures from him without divulging anything of her own, but she didn't feel up to confessions at the moment. At the moment she was too taken up with trying to resist the urge to clasp her arms

118

about him and press her mouth into the tanned column of his neck.

He seemed to accept her reticence, merely stretching out onto his back and watching the few clouds wafting past overhead. After a while she stretched out beside him within a fingertip of his reach.

"I used to dream about days like this," he said lazily. "Dream of being wrapped in sunshine and silence, allowed to have a moment of my very own, to luxuriate in the fresh smell of the air. And the colors. To share the colors, living colors, not something on a movie screen or magazine page, but something I could reach out and touch. That first day back I felt deluged by all the colors, the clothes, the shop signs, the cars, and the billboards. I felt as if I'd fallen inside a rainbow and was drowning in a flood of color."

His tone was such a fusion of contentment and yearning that Beth knew another piercing of her soul. What must it be like, to yearn for something as ordinary as color? To dream of privacy the way most people dream of riches? The thought of it made her ache. The thought of Kaler yearning and dreaming for such things made her ache with special poignancy.

"You make my old dreams sound mundane," she said.

He rolled his head around to look at her. "And what exactly did you dream about?"

"Oh, all the usual things. A husband, a home, babies."

His heart began pounding. "Do you still dream of those things, Beth?"

She raised her hand to cover her eyes, as if from the sun, but actually from his probing gaze. "Oh, no, not these days. Now I dream of actually getting my desk cleared off, just once, if even for only ten minutes."

"Now, that's what I can't make fit about you," he said.

"What?"

"Why aren't you married, with the home and the ba-

119

bies of your dreams? It doesn't make sense to me. Don't the men around here have eyes in their heads? How could they let you get away?"

He seemed determined to press the point. She was equally determined not to discuss it. This had been such a lovely afternoon, she didn't want thoughts of Lance to spoil it.

"You make me sound," she complained peevishly, "like a prize bass. Nobody let me get away because I'm not a catch. I'm a person, not a fish."

Though she'd meant to tease him, her words carried a stridency that caught Kaler up short. The last thing he meant to do was antagonize her for any reason. He should have known better than to pry, no one knew better than he how distressing unwanted probing could be. He thought perhaps it was time to end this idyllic spell before he once again snapped the slender thread of communication between them. Sitting upright, he stretched, then said as easily as he could, "I know I was away from women for a long time, but believe me, it wasn't so long that I can't tell the difference between a woman and a fish."

She flushed. "Sorry."

His laughter was as warm and mellow as the buttery sunshine coating them. "No problem." He stretched again. He was stalling and he knew it. But each moment with her seemed so precious, so filled with the companionship he'd yearned for throughout all the long, lonely, lost years, he wanted to linger over every sweet second he spent with her. Especially here, with the freedom and the solitude and the prairie he'd so craved in all the years of captivity. He felt as if he could stay on this haystack with her for all time and be happy. But in the end, he did what he had to.

"I hate to say it, but I think it's time for us to go back," he said reluctantly.

"I guess so," she said with equal reluctance.

Any hope that she'd insist they stay longer was snuffed and Kaler accepted the inevitable. His idyll was over.

CHAPTER NINE

He half-jumped, half-slid to the ground. Turning, he saw Beth leap. Instinctively his arms shot out and he lunged forward. She crashed against his chest, sending them both toppling with a heavy thud. Cradling her in his arms, he landed flat on his back. Her white hairclip flew past his shoulder into the stubble and her hair cascaded over his cheeks. They lay motionless, heartbeat to heartbeat.

Gradually, almost of its own volition, his hand came up. His fingertips delicately grazed her cheek as he tenderly brushed back the silken blond strands. His heart thudded. Her lips were but a breath away.

"Are you hurt?" he asked unsteadily.

She knew she should get off him. But she was curiously loath to move a single muscle. Nestled against the warmth of his body, she felt all her inhibitions melting away. "No," she assured him on a faint sigh.

Her murmur kissed his jaw. He drew in his breath sharply and her lowered lashes fluttered upward. Her eyes were a darker shade of blue than he'd ever seen them. Dark and liquid and enflaming. Shuddering, he fought against his surging need to kiss her, to touch her, to mold the soft contours of her body to the hard imprint of his own. Any other woman, and he swore to God he'd take her then and there. But this was Beth, his special friend, the one woman he could not have. And the only one he wanted.

Kaler had long since learned the bitter lessons of self-control, but never had the lesson been so cruel. Never had he been so tempted to reject the constraints as he was now, totally captivated by her. But he knew how everyone else would view any relationship between them and he could not, he would not, subject her to such censure. Through sheer force of will, he clamped his jaw tight and clenched his fists at his sides. He closed his eyes to shut out the entrancement of her.

But the warm weight of her, the delicate scent of her, the intimate flexure of her, continued to torment him. White-hot need set his loins afire.

With a butterfly touch Beth skimmed a fingertip down his rigid cheekbone. She heard his ragged breath and saw his dilated eyes widen further still. Settled as intimately as she was, she was fully aware of his arousal. Seeing his taut expression, feeling his tensed muscles, she was fully aware that he was resisting his feelings. She was fully aware that she must stop exciting him. But her conscience was overwhelmed by her intense need to explore the wonders of him, to know the splendor of his body beneath her hands. Her passion trampled her scruples and left the fragments in the stubble of the field.

She rested the pad of her finger against the corner of his mouth and felt the moist heat of his low groan. It was a sensual mouth, full, with a deeply masculine indentation; desire careened in her veins and she could not resist the temptation to trace the curve of it.

"Beth," he moaned hoarsely.

Lightly she twirled her finger along the edge of his teeth. She felt peculiarly detached from her actions, as if some other woman possessed that gossamer stroke, someone else beguiled him so provocatively.

He must tell her to stop. She didn't know, she couldn't

understand the shattering force of her effect. Kaler opened his mouth to speak, and instead, gently closed his lips upon her finger, playing his tongue against the tip.

But in his mind his tongue sketched the puckered nipple of her breast, savoring the grainy texture.

Knowing he must set her away while he still could, he brought his hands to rest on her sides. His thumbs glanced over the soft suggestion of her breasts and his grip tightened against her rib cage.

But in his mind his palms filled with the pliant softness, the buds firming to his persuasive caress.

He lay beneath her, full and aching, straining to curb his excitement, willing himself not to lift his hand higher, not to trail his mouth from fingertip to palm to wrist and beyond.

Mentally he held her without restraint, his hands and lips seeking freely, feverishly, as their bodies twined together. Supple, silken, exquisitely responsive—she was all these things and more, in his mind.

He gasped. The images pulsed through him with consuming intensity. With one swift motion Kaler tumbled Beth to the ground. As she gaped at him in wide-eyed shock, he bolted upright and sucked in slow, deep, steadying gulps of air.

Beth blinked at him. She had known he was aroused, she couldn't help but know, but her own arousal had obscured how very intensely he'd been stirred. All she had done was touch his cheek, his lips. She would never have imagined such a painfully impassioned response. But his desire was obvious in his tense features, his still-trembling body. Heavy remorse burdened her for the way in which she had teased him.

"Kaler, I'm sorry, I never meant—"

"Don't, just don't, Beth. It's over, forget it."

He sounded so harsh, she felt even worse. She hung her

head, her hair tangling about her shoulders. "But I am sorry, Kaler. I should never have—"

"You never should have jumped like that from the haystack," he interrupted brusquely. "You could have been hurt."

She knew she should never have done a lot more than that, but decided not to say so. The least said, the soonest mended, seemed to be the most appropriate maxim to follow. She rose on shaky legs and swept bits of clinging straw from her body. She spoke in a hurried staccato that matched the agitation of her hands. "I always jump down like that. I've never once hurt myself, not even my ankle. Isn't that absurd? I can hurt that darn ankle just tripping over a breeze. I should've warned you I was coming, but it honestly never occurred to me—"

"Beth," he said, and this time he was like a gentling mist, softly hushed and soothing.

She stood stock-still. Her body drummed with each agonizing beat of her heart as she slowly raised her gaze to meet his. The hint of a rueful smile indented his full mouth; the silvered passion lingered in his eyes.

"It's all right, Beth," he comforted her. "You couldn't know."

Never had she felt such a welling of emotion as she did now. She thought she would drown in the flood of guilt, relief, joy, and indefinable caring that poured forth.

"You couldn't help it," he went on, measuring each word before producing it. "It wasn't anything you did. It was . . . it's been so long since . . . just being near"— he nearly said *you,* but managed in time to say—"a woman . . . can excite me. It wasn't really you at all."

It was the biggest lie of all time. She was the only woman he'd ever really wanted, really wanted in such a soul-stirring way. But of course, he'd never be able to tell her that.

All her emotions drained away, leaving only an uncertain injured pique. The thought of someone else arousing him in such a way rankled her. She looked at him with that mixture of hurt and anger rigidly imprinted on her features.

He recognized that harsh expression; he'd read condemnation in too many faces not to know it when he saw it. The crystalline fragility of his hopes splintered into shards that pierced his soul. "I swear I won't touch you again," he said grimly.

Irrationally, this irritated her further still. Stiffening, her face stonily set, she suggested they forget about it. "As soon as I find my clip, we can get going," she finished on a note to match her hardened mien.

Every little shard wound its way to the center of his being. He wanted to cry out, to tell her he couldn't bear having her turn away from him. But pride kept him mute. He bent to help in her search for the hair clip, but could not see for the pain blurring his vision.

"Here it is," she said, straightening. Scooping the clip as well as the bag into her hand, she did not wait to redo her hair, but strode off through the field. He had no option but to follow.

They walked the shade-speckled path in single file, silent, oblivious to the whispering cottonwood trees, the racketing chorus of unseen creatures, the checkering sunlight. Both were too immersed in emotional reflection to pay attention to anything else.

Kaler suffered an agonizing inner upheaval. The time with Beth was cherished, a memory to treasure and sustain him in his loneliness. But it was also a bitterly cruel reminder of all that he'd never had, of all the years without someone who cared, someone to share with, someone to shine a light against the darkness of his life. He knew he was totally unacceptable for someone as sweet and good as Beth. He wasn't the sort of man women like Beth could love. That she'd even given him her sympathy and concern had moved him beyond measure. He certainly didn't expect anything more. But having known the joy and the contentment of even that small gift, he didn't think he could bear going on with anything less.

He was well-acquainted with pain. He'd known all kinds of pain—that of desertion, of denial, of dehumanization. But he'd never before known the gut-wrenching pain of a loss like this. Without Beth, without her gentle kindness to ease his days, his empty life would be more starkly barren than he could bear. Already the desolation shrouded his soul.

Beth was not so clear about what she felt. Her emotions were muddled, a chaotic tangle that defied unraveling. The one thread she'd seemed able to cling to was her distress over being lumped together with all the women who could excite him. The notion disturbed her in myriad ways. It depressed and annoyed her; it bruised her ego, offended her sensibilities. *It wasn't really you,* he'd said and she'd wanted to shriek, *Why not?* She didn't want to be *a* woman who affected him so strongly, she wanted to be the only woman.

Her step faltered. My God, what was she thinking? She swiftly regained her step and proceeded, thankful he could not see her expression. A ringing box on the ears could not have stunned her more. The unexpected revelation was all the more astounding for its veracity.

She didn't waste a second doubting it; the truth was obvious in the sudden dancing of her nerves. She'd always been attracted to him, she'd come to like and respect him, she was certain it would be all too easy to feel a great deal more for him. But still she shied away from the thought of letting herself feel that something more. Love meant opening yourself up to another, to making yourself vulnerable to the searing pain of disillusionment. She had vowed never to be so vulnerable again. Was she possibly ready now to take the risk? Was she ready to

127

take a chance on her tumultuous feelings for Kaler? She didn't know. She just didn't know if she could again endure the type of emotional devastation Lance had put her through.

One thing she did know, however, was that she owed Kaler an apology. She'd behaved badly, teasing him to satisfy her needs without a thought for his. Then she'd compounded her guilt by venting her vexation at him when all he'd done was to try to make her feel better. Her childish behavior had spoiled the halcyon perfection of their afternoon together and though no amount of apologies could restore it, she had to let him know how very sorry she was.

As soon as they came to the edge of the grassy path she took in a deep breath and half-turned. A stamping of feet interrupted her before she could speak. She whirled to see Dale and Ted running toward them. She sensed Kaler's immediate defensive stance and prayed this day would not get any worse. But her prayer went unanswered.

"What's going on here?" Dale demanded, a belligerent scowl darkening his normally pleasant features.

With as calm a manner as she could muster under the circumstances, which, with two brothers glowering fiercely at her head-on and one O'Connell radiating hostile strength at her back, weren't too serene, she inquired, "Why, Dale, what can you mean?"

"What are you doing here with *him?*" he growled. His jaw thrust pugnaciously forward, he glared at Kaler.

Beth peered over her shoulder and nearly shuddered. It was worse than she'd feared. Kaler stood with his feet planted apart, his head cocked slightly as he sent her brother a look that would wither a plant to its roots. A tacit challenge was boldly clear in his stance, his attitude. This was the old Kaler, and she wasn't at all sure she wanted to have anything to do with him. From the militant noises Dale was making, however, it was all too clear

128

he would thoroughly enjoy having something to do with Kaler. She sent a silent appeal to her youngest brother, but Ted, usually so much more temperate, mirrored Dale's apparent readiness for a fight. Her heart sinking, she said on a resigned sigh, "We've been walking."

"Walking!" Dale exploded.

"With *him?*" Ted shouted.

She stiffened. They made it sound as if she'd do better to walk with Jack the Ripper. "Is there some problem?" she asked coldly.

Dale ignored her. Facing Kaler, he issued a terse order. "Stay away from my sister, O'Connell."

Kaler would have liked nothing better than to release some of his pent-up pain and frustration in a fight. For one fleeting fraction of a second he nearly listened to his pumping adrenaline and let his fists swing. But he hadn't spent the past seven weeks trying to turn his life around to throw it all away in one angry moment. He kept his mouth shut and his fists at his sides.

"She doesn't need the likes of you bothering her."

"Honestly, Dale, I'm not a child!" Beth burst out. It was clearly evident that her brother intended to provoke a fight and she was now utterly furious with him. The hair clip bit into her curled palm as she stated incisively, "I'm perfectly capable of deciding with whom I wish to walk."

Dale threw her a frown of pure disgust. "That's debatable," he muttered.

She longed to turn him over her knee and spank him, which was a suitably childish punishment for his incredibly childish behavior. But even more, she wanted to get Kaler away before a fight truly did erupt. She couldn't have borne it if anything she did resulted in his parole being revoked. Turning to address Kaler, she said with warm sincerity, "I'm sorry you've been subjected to this rude display of bad manners, Kaler. I assure you my

129

brother, both my brothers, generally show more courtesy, if not more sense."

Alert to her every flick of expression, Kaler could read the storm still enraging her and his admiration for her control gave him the impetus to respond in kind. "That's all right. It's understandable, given the circumstances. I believe it would be best if I left—"

"You're darn right it would be best!" Dale interjected.

Beth flashed him a deadly look before presenting Kaler with her prettiest smile, the one Lance had always called dazzling. "I don't blame you for wanting to get away, but you won't forget our date tonight, will you? I promise you I'll be there promptly at seven."

He understood her motivation; she'd been goaded into this, but Kaler was quick to grasp at the chance she offered him to rectify all the transgressions of the afternoon. Besides, in the brilliancy of that smile, he'd have agreed to anything. Without the least hesitation, he nodded. "I won't forget. Meet you outside the Starlite, right?"

"Right," she said, and a giddy thrill weakened her knees.

Explosive little squawks of shock sparked between her brothers, igniting Dale, who fired a shrill "Are you crazy?" at her.

"You could still wait for the ride," said Beth to Kaler, paying no attention at all to either brother.

"I really do prefer to walk," he said.

"I'll see you at seven then."

"You'll be okay?"

"I can handle them," she assured him.

A smile, soft and knowing, passed between them. For Kaler, it brought renewed hope. For Beth, it brought another jumbling of her already disordered emotions.

With a fervent gratitude to the antagonistic brothers who'd inadvertently given him another chance, Kaler strode away. Beth followed him with hungry eyes, her vision spellbound by the memory of his body beneath hers. He moved with an unmatched grace, the splendid shifting of bone and muscle summoning up the superlative feel of them, enkindling suggestions of the excitement of them, of him.

The instant he disappeared around the corner of the shed, she was yanked back to her senses. Ted and Dale clamored at her, demanding to know if she'd lost her mind, her sense, her morals, until she felt she had to speak or be smothered in the avalanche of their accusations.

"I can't imagine," she drawled in a restrained tone, "what my morals have to do with it. We're going on a date, not a heist."

"How can you make jokes about this!"

Maybe her mother was right; maybe the hospital had made a mistake. What other explanation could there be for a brother like Dale? She sighed audibly. "I joke because if I didn't lighten my mood a bit, I'd be seriously tempted to run you through with the nearest pitchfork."

"You're not going out with that jailbird," snarled Dale resolutely.

"What right have you got to interfere in my life?" she snapped. "What right have you got to insult my guests?"

"We didn't mean to be rude, Beth." Ted's freckled face didn't bear any of his normal cheer; from his blue eyes to his downturned mouth, he looked worried. "But it was such a shock, seeing you with O'Connell, that we just sort of blew up."

"I still don't see that it's any of your business."

"We care about you, Beth," Dale said almost irritably. "And we're concerned about you. If we interfere, it's only for your own good."

She covered her face with her hands. She was no longer certain whether she was infuriated, amused, or

131

both. It seemed no matter where she went or what she did, she couldn't escape the misguided but sincere desire to protect her from herself. It was a conspiracy of concern that was driving her crazy. Amusement won out. She dropped her hands, raised her eyes heavenward, and intoned gravely, "Dear Lord, please save me from all these fools who wish to run my life for my own good."

Dale sputtered. "Okay, okay, make jokes about it. Why should I waste my time worrying if you don't."

"My point precisely," said Beth decisively. "Now, if you'll excuse me, I've a date to get ready for."

She darted away before they could find new ammunition to fire at her. Glancing back, she saw them, their heads shaking as they conferred together—more than likely, she thought wryly, on whether a jacket or a net would be more effective. Once hidden from view by the barn and sheds, she broke out into a run, the plastic bag bumping against her knee and her hair flying out in an unruly mass behind her. She ran to the pounding beat of her heart. Each step rang in her ears with the message that pursued her.

She was going out with Kaler on a real date!

She dashed up the back steps and was halfway through the kitchen when she realized her mother had said something. She spun to a halt. "What, Mom?"

"I only wondered if you felt it necessary to use the kitchen as a racetrack or were doing so only on a whim," said Emma, not missing a stroke of her paring knife on the potato she held.

"Sorry, but I'm in a hurry."

"Oh? I hadn't noticed." She paused then and pointed with the blade of her knife toward the counter opposite the sink where she stood. "By the way, Beth, you left your book in here. I'm sorry, I didn't mean to pry, but I wondered what it was doing there and read the inscription by mistake."

132

Her tone was utterly without inflection. A tingle tracked up Beth's spine at the deliberate lack of expression. She came slowly into the work area of the kitchen. Her mother resumed her interest in her potato, keeping her back to her daughter. Beth sent her a silent thanks as she lifted the copy of *The Prophet* from the counter beside the stove and opened it. She hadn't bothered to do so before, and as she turned to the flyleaf, she was rather glad she hadn't read this in front of Kaler.

In an unadorned script, he'd written: To BETH, SOMETHING I ADMIRE FOR SOMEONE I ADMIRE. KALER.

Trembling, she closed the book. She glanced at her mother's slim back, her slenderness emphasized by the black slacks and blouse. She looked more like a thin silhouette than an actual person and Beth knew another burst of gratitude. If her mother had said one word, just one, the pleasure of it would have been marred. It was a joy too special to be shared.

She silently picked up the book and headed back toward the door. She paused there. "By the way," she said with studied nonchalance, "I won't be home for dinner tonight."

Emma raised her head to look across at her daughter. "Oh?"

"I have a date, a dinner date," she said. After a thudding heartbeat, she added, "With Kaler."

"Oh," her mother said again. Then Emma smiled before returning to her work.

It was enough. Encouraged by her mother, uplifted by the message, Beth skipped upstairs. Her brothers' animosity was forgotten and her own guilt of the afternoon was washed away.

Sitting in the oak rocker that faced the window in her bedroom, she reopened the book and again read the notation Kaler had written. Just seeing his handwriting sent

133

quivers spiraling through her. She traced each word with her fingers and remembered how she'd traced the line of his cheek. And she remembered his shuddering breath, his rampaging heartbeat, his undeniable arousal. All from a single touch.

But he'd said he'd react the same with any woman.

She pressed her hand against the page, imprinting her palm with his words and imagining the heat of his skin kissing her flesh. The memory of his warmth quivered within her. With such delicate deliberation she had touched him, savoring each inch of the firm bone and textured skin. With equal deliberation she had separated herself from what she now recognized as an attempted seduction. And his body had pulsed from the force of it.

He'd said it wasn't anything she'd done.

She leaned her head back and closed her eyes. "You make a lousy vamp, Rasmussen."

He had sworn not to touch her again.

She recalled the lambent smile they'd shared before he left and she half-laughed, half-sobbed.

"Oh, Kaler," she whispered. "Oh, Kaler, I want you to touch me again. I don't want it to be the same with anyone else. I want it to be special with me. I want to be the one to make you shine. Kaler, Kaler, I don't want you to admire me, I want you to love me."

She wanted it as surely as she breathed. She wanted it because, ready for the risk or not, she loved him. She loved Kaler O'Connell.

CHAPTER TEN

The Starlite Café was famous for its onion rings and
homemade rhubarb pie. Tart and greasy odors hung permanently in the air, clinging to the red vinyl chairs and
saturating the crimson tablecloths. The decor was limited
to a potted Norfolk pine that stood beside the cash regis-
ter counter and a community bulletin board on which
notices of sales, jobs wanted or needed, baby-sitters, free
puppies, and local events were haphazardly plastered.
The lighting was dingy, the noise discordant. Despite all
that, the Starlite was never empty, particularly on Saturday nights, when a sizable portion of the town descended
upon its dining room to fill up on good food and neigh-
borly conversation.

A steady stream flowed in and out of the restaurant.
Some distance away, beneath the orange and black
striped awning of Dorothy's Dresses, Kaler stood watching the diners come and go. He was aware of each sidelong look, each inimical whisper, each hurried footstep
going past him. There was a time when he'd have met the
look with an arrogant curl of his lip, interrupted the
whisper with an insolent suggestion that the speakers
take a flying leap, and stepped brazenly in front of those
scurrying to get out of his way, issuing a challenge that
didn't need words. That was long ago, another lifetime,
another man. Now he did his best to fade into the shad-

ows, to suppress the deep desire to respond as he always had, with anger and arrogance and a pretense that he didn't give a damn. He did his best to ignore the hurt.

It wasn't possible. Each time he caught another censorious glance cast his way, he thought of Beth. He didn't think he could restrain himself if anyone looked at Beth that way. And they would; he knew they would. If she were with him, she'd become part of the target. Worse, because she'd be with him, he'd have no choice. He'd have to restrain himself.

He shoved his fists into the pockets of his wheaten slacks and stared down at the cracked pavement. He'd told her he'd come back because of the prairie, but there were other prairies. Pride, not the prairie, had compelled him to return home. This was the place he had to prove himself. These were the people he had to show he'd changed. But even knowing how tough it would be didn't make it any easier to deal with the constant condemnation. Some days he felt like a recovering alcoholic, taking only one day at a time, reining in his hurt and resentment day by day. He felt as if he were being continually tested, but never received a grade.

The squeal of girlish giggles arrested his musings. He looked up before he could stop himself. A trio of teenagers bedecked in an array of kaleidoscopic polka dots, stripes, and checks gawked, then bent their heads together for a conclave of zealous chattering. An unfriendly breeze carried the taunting hiss of the words he most hated: prison, con, crook. Within his pockets his balled fists tightened.

And he knew with certainty that he could not subject Beth to this.

Pivoting on his heel, he strode at a clip guaranteed to get him as far away as possible before she turned up. She probably wouldn't show up anyway. It was already after

136

seven. She hadn't really wanted to go out with him; she'd been spurred into it by her brothers.

He stepped into the street. A horn blared, brakes shrieked, and a tan compact swerved directly onto his path. He lurched to a stop. Automatically every muscle tensed, alert, poised for trouble. His eyes narrowed, he looked down.

"What are you doing? The Starlite's the other way!" Beth's cornsilk hair tossed in the wind as she poked her head out the window to frown up at him.

"I know," he said tightly.

"Is it because I'm late?" She smiled crookedly, contritely. "I'm sorry, but Jenny just got home. I was ready to wring her neck, I was so furious. And parking's a premium around here on Saturday night, so I was—"

An angry horn and a shout interrupted her flowing explanation. She checked the car behind her, then gestured at Kaler. "Get in and we'll talk while I look for a place to park."

Another imperious trumpeting terminated his hesitation. He darted around to the passenger side and even before he shut the door they were moving. He closed his eyes and let his relief seep into every pore. She had come. He only now realized how much he'd longed she would.

"As I was saying before we were so rudely interrupted, I'm sorry I was late." She stole a peek at him. "But I wasn't really all that late. Why were you leaving?"

He straightened, then looked at her. For a moment he couldn't breathe, much less speak. She wore a dress unlike any he'd seen on her at work—a soft, summery sort of dress with thin straps and a V-neck and almost no back at all. The turquoise skirt was full yet clingy, hugging the shape of her thighs as he himself longed to do. Somehow he forced himself to look away.

"I realized," he said in a monotone, "that it would be best if we forgot the whole thing."

137

"Forgot it? Why?"

"You don't have to go through with this, Beth. I know you suggested we go out only in order to goad your brothers. That's why I went along with it. I didn't really expect you to show up, and when you were late, well—"

"I do not consider a measly fifteen minutes late," she broke in frostily.

Before he could respond she swung into a parking spot and jerked to a halt. She faced him, and for the first time he saw a distinct resemblance of Beth to her contumacious brother Dale. With her chin thrust up, she stated emphatically, "Whatever the reason, we agreed to go out tonight. I was glad about it. Obviously you're not. Is it my breath? Or are you ashamed to be seen with me?"

"How could you even suggest—"

"What else am I to believe? That you think I'll be ashamed of you? That says a lot about what you think of me, doesn't it?"

"You don't understand how they'll look at you, how they'll talk. I don't want to subject you to that."

She stared at him for a very long time. Long enough for him to notice the faint dusting of blue shadow on her eyelids, the mascara darkening her fair lashes. Long enough for him to realize she'd taken the trouble to look her best tonight. Long enough to wonder why.

At length she sighed, a drawn-out expulsion that reeked of disappointment. "You know, I would never have figured you to be the sort to run away."

A plunge into an ice bath would have been less effective. After a startled second in which he gaped dumfounded, Kaler closed his mouth with a snap and ejected himself from the car. She did not move until he'd yanked open her door. Then she slid out with a knowingly triumphant smile.

The blocks to the Starlite were covered in bustling silence. Kaler's anger with her scarcely lasted beyond the first step; he knew she was right, he couldn't run away. Wasn't that why he'd come back to Pasque in the first place? But he didn't feel he could speak or slow down or he'd lose his courage to go through the restaurant door. Worried on his behalf more than her own, Beth kept silent and kept pace. For his sake, for their sake, she hoped she'd done the right thing by impelling him into this.

Inside, the babble of voices fell for several stunned seconds, then rose with renewed vigor. They walked a gauntlet of stares to a table near the back. A tight ball of anger wound within Kaler's stomach, twisting more tightly with each sneering whisper he heard. He couldn't tolerate exposing Beth to the barbs he routinely received. As soon as they sat down he said flatly, "I don't think this was such a good idea."

She took one look at his taut jaw and decided he was right. But they were here and Beth wasn't a quitter. "It's a great idea. I've a weakness for their onion rings."

"I'm not really hungry," he said.

"My mouth's been watering all evening."

"I think we should go."

"We just sat down and I'm hungry, even if you're not. Besides, it's my treat."

This proved to be a striking diversionary statement. He frowned and said, "Of course it's not. It's a date. I'm paying."

"As you pointed out earlier, it's not a real date. I put you on the spot, pressing you into this just to annoy Dale and Ted. Therefore, I should pay."

"No, you shouldn't. You're not," he said.

She gave him her "Emma" look. "I should and I am. Or, at least," she amended hastily, taking in his glowering disapproval, "I'm paying half. We'll go dutch, how's that?"

He didn't like it and told her so, but when she threat-

139

ened to add him to her list of known MCPs, he agreed to it. "God knows, I'm on enough 'known' lists," he added.

She glanced at him sharply, but to her relief he was smiling crookedly. She grinned and shot back, "If you don't like dutch treats, you'll just have to ask me out properly next time."

His whole being cheered with the thought of there being a next time.

They ordered a double burger and a tenderloin with extra mayo plus a platter of the infamous onion rings, and conversed about work as they ate. Kaler began to relax. It was part of Beth's specialness, this ability to untighten the coil of tension within him. Beth, in turn, felt her spirit lighten as she sensed his mood mellowing. It was part of her newly discovered love, this finding joy in his joy. Immersed as they were in each other, they didn't realize someone had approached them until they were addressed. Or rather, Beth was addressed.

"Um, hello, Beth," said Gail Walkingstick with nervous hesitation.

"Hello, Gail," she replied, smiling. "You know Kaler O'Connell, don't you?"

Carefully avoiding looking in his direction, Gail waved her hand toward the table where her husband sat. "Uh, well, anyway, Roy and I just wondered if everything is okay?"

Beth stiffened. She glanced at all two hundred and fifty pounds of Roy. She gave him a tight smile, then transferred it to Gail. "Well, the tenderloin was a bit overfried, but the rings were as terrific as ever."

Gail had the grace to blush. She murmured a quick "Catch you at the next meeting," and scurried back to her table. Seeing the grim set of Kaler's face, Beth rather wished she'd told Gail what she thought of her and had booted her on her ample rump to emphasize the point.

140

She put her sandwich down. "This tenderloin really is overfried," she said too cheerily. "How's the burger?"

"You're going to lose friends over this, Beth," he said.

"Don't worry about me, Kaler. I'm perfectly capable of handling a few snubs."

"You don't know how vindictive people can be. You're so good, you don't expect the worst from others, but—"

"But if you keep this up, you'll see the worst from me," she broke in, only half-teasing. "You don't need to protect me. Not only do I feel that I'm capable enough on my own, I assure you I get more than enough over-protection from my family."

She could see she hadn't convinced him. Frustrated, still annoyed with Gail's well-meaning but aggravating interruption, she stabbed an onion ring into the ketchup. A squirt of red sauce spurted upward and splattered the front of his bone-white shirt. For a second she stared at the stain in horror, then she dipped the end of her napkin in her water and reached across the table to dab at it.

"I'm so sorry, Kaler! I should have been more careful!"

He stayed her agitated hand. As much as he'd have enjoyed her ministrations—he'd always longed for some-one to fuss over him in all the little, tender ways—he didn't want to toss any more fuel into the speculative fire he could see in those around them. He pried the napkin from her grip and dampened the spot on his shirt. "Now this, I'm sure, would be a prime example of what my old cellmate always called the boomerang effect," he re-marked with a solemn frown.

"Boomerang effect?"

"Anger always comes back at you," he explained.

"But you're the one who got ketchup all over your shirt," she pointed out.

"Because I was furious with that woman for spoiling our evening." His frown slid crookedly into a sheepish smile and her heart tilted with it.

The words rushed to the tip of her tongue, she longed to say them, she longed to tell him she loved him, but instead, she said, "She hasn't spoiled our evening. It would take a lot more than that to spoil it. At least for me."

He looked at her and all the stares blurred, all the whispers muted. So long as she smiled at him like that, with such tender caring, he couldn't see or hear anything else. He wanted to tell her how much her smile meant to him, how much *she* meant to him. But he still had difficulty expressing his gentler feelings, even with her. It seemed impossible for him to find a way to say what he felt so deeply.

Shoving aside the remains of his burger, he said simply, "I'm ready to get out of here," and when she concurred, he signaled for their waitress. They got a doggie bag for the remainder of the rings, paid, and left. And as they walked out, Beth quite deliberately set her hand on Kaler's arm. She left it there as they walked down the street.

"I'm beginning to believe," he drawled, "that there's a real streak of rebellion in you after all."

She laughed and merrily claimed an "I told you so." He thought, *So this is what happiness is like, this elated feeling of fulfillment.*

They strolled slowly, enjoying the lowering sun as it warmed the summer dusk. Their images wavered on store windows, flickering amid pharmaceutical goods and the coming fall fashions and baseball bats at half price. Glimpsing the reflection of the couple strolling arm in arm, Kaler knew a wistful yearning that the reality would outlast the image. He firmly tamped down the sadness and lost himself in the enjoyment of the moment.

Her skirt rustled softly, femininely. He imagined the gentle hush of it beneath his palm. Her hair whisked in the playful breeze. He pictured the silken gold of it threaded about his fingers. Her fragrance wafted on the air tantalizingly. He envisioned the sweetness of it upon his lips as he pressed his mouth against the pulse of her throat. When they reached her car, that wistful sadness again impinged on his contentment. He didn't want it to end, he wanted to linger in the bittersweet fantasy of her.

"It's a nice evening," he said, stalling. "Not so muggy."

It seemed a beautiful evening to Beth, but she simply murmured, "Yes, it is," and offered him an onion ring. He took it and they leaned against the side of her car while they wordlessly munched. She ate as slowly as she could, but still it seemed the onion rings vanished too quickly. She dusted crumbs from her lips, caught Kaler watching her intently, and said on a flustered note, "Well, I guess it's time to go."

He reluctantly agreed, but as soon as they got into her car he realized he couldn't let the evening end so quickly. "I know a great spot for viewing the sunset," he said. "You interested?"

"Absolutely," she answered with wholehearted truth. She felt relieved. She'd been trying desperately to think of a way to ask to see his etchings.

Following his directions, she drove out of town, off the major highway, rambled over several country backroads, and finally came to a small grove of trees that ringed a white cube of a building with boarded-up windows and a wooden X barring the door. A black iron bell swung silently from a hook at the front, a narrow outhouse leaned lopsidedly at a discreet distance in the back.

"I'd forgotten all about this place," exclaimed Beth. She beamed joyfully at him.

"I rediscovered it on my walks," he explained. He didn't say that he'd gone looking for it. In the long-ago days it had been his place of solace. He'd broken into the

143

building more times than he could count, simply to sit in the cool dark solitude.

"It was still in use when I was a kid," she said, "and I looked forward to coming here. But it closed the year I started school. It took me months to get over my disappointment."

"It used to be where I brought girls to make out," he said with a rakish grin.

She lowered her lashes and peered at him coquettishly. "Used to be, you say?" she murmured.

His heart did a backflip. He couldn't believe she could be flirting with him. The mere thought of it accelerated his heartbeat. He thrust open his door. "Let's go sit out in the breeze."

Three cracked steps led up to the concrete slab porch. They sat side by side, carefully not touching. Leaves danced through the trees, locusts whirred in a cacophonous harmony. The sky lit softly with streaks of rose and peachblow. Dusk settled peacefully over them.

Beth felt the air cooling her skin. Unreasonably, her blood began warming. He was so close, so achingly close. A stretch of her finger and she would know how the twilight air sat upon his arm. She peeked sidelong at him. "And so, did you?" she asked, her voice unusually husky.

"Did I what?"

"Make out. You know, with all those girls you brought here."

"My God, the questions you ask."

She aimlessly twirled a strand of hair on her finger and drawled, "You had quite the rep back then. O'Connell, the lady-killer. The girls' room at the high school was littered with graffiti about you."

"My hall of fame," he said with a twisted smile.

"It was all highly complimentary, I assure you." She flashed him a coy grin. "Of course, you have to take into account that bathroom graffiti is notoriously exaggerated.

144

Still, speculation about your . . . prowess . . . was widespread. And every time a girl turned up pregnant, we—"

She stopped cold. What in hell was she saying? She chanced a look. He was staring at the toe of his shoe, his face the expressionless mask she so hated. Thinking she should have her mouth taped permanently shut, she finished on a shaky whisper, "But it was never you."

The diffusing twilight glossed his dark hair as he shook his head. "The last thing I would ever do is bring another unwanted child into the world."

Sorrow spun a web within her soul. She wished she could tell him she was sorry, that she hadn't meant to be so insensitive, but she somehow knew an apology would simply make things worse. The past held such a grip on the present, at times it seemed to her to be a deathlock.

Kaler understood her disquiet, and the reason for it. The need to comfort her overrode any dejection he himself felt whenever he thought of his past. He leaned back on his elbows, bent a knee upward, and said with lazy intimation, "As far as I can recall, I never saw your number scrawled in the boys' room. You were obviously one of the saintly types who held out for marriage."

A searching look told her he wasn't simply trying to be valiant. He appeared very much at ease. A bit of her own tension diminished. "With a family like mine, I had little choice," she said lightly. "You've seen how protective they can be. When I was a teenager I felt positively smothered."

"You bring a lot of it on yourself," he said, and she instantly demanded to know how. "You just have that way about you; you look as if you need protecting, need someone to look out for you."

He refrained from suggesting that he be that someone. Tension rebounded, redoubled in force. She contemplated the permutations of the sky from blue to purple-

145

pink to a fading gray and the hint of sapphire to come, and wondered whether she could tell him. The decision was pre-set. If she wanted any sort of real relationship with him, she had to expose her vulnerabilities. She had to risk the hurt and disappointment to gain the joyful contentment that only being loved by the one you love can bring.

"I think maybe you're right," she said at last. "Even when I went to college, people always seemed to watch out for me. But then, it was a small school, the kind where you know everyone on campus and they all know you. Sometimes it seemed as if I were still in high school."

He could sense the buildup to something important. Willing himself to sound casual, he remarked, "You said once you went into teaching."

"Yes. In Minneapolis." This was her moment, but she wasn't at all certain how to proceed. In the end, she tossed her hurt out with a saucy, "Which is where I fell from sainthood."

Kaler said nothing, for which she was grateful. Having made the plunge, she decided to go ahead and swim. "He was a teacher at my school. He was everything all the guys back home had never been—cosmopolitan, sophisticated, cultured. Plus he was great with kids; the children all adored him. I tumbled completely." She grimaced. "Lousy choice of words, but highly accurate. Because the school restricted involvement between teachers, all our meetings were clandestine, hurried. It was only after I was well and truly involved that I learned he was married."

It cost him no little effort, but Kaler managed not to spit out the crude descriptives with which he was castigating the man who'd hurt her so.

"Of course I instantly broke it off." She laughed, a sour little laugh that left a bad taste in her mouth. "My attack

146

of scruples didn't last long. When the next school year started, little by little, it all started up again—the meetings, the weekends, the rushed gropings. I hated myself. But I loved him, or thought I did. So I continued to see him."

She hung her head. Her hair shimmered golden in the descending darkness. He longed to brush it back with a soothing hand, to hold her within the comfort of his embrace.

"It went on all year, but at the end of the year I demanded he leave his wife. He just stared, then asked where on earth I'd ever gotten the idea that he would leave his wife. The notion truly shocked him. I felt sick, shamed, and hurt. I wasn't able to cope, so in the end, I came home."

It took all her courage, but she raised her eyes to his. "Oh, Kaler, don't you see? I let it go on a year, a full year, after I knew he was married. How can you possibly think I'm good or sweet? Now you must think I'm little better than a—"

He shushed her in the swiftest, most effective way he knew. He wrapped her within his arms and silenced her mouth with his own.

CHAPTER ELEVEN

Gentle, undemanding, a gift of solace, his kiss calmed her. She relaxed within his embrace, luxuriating in the comforting strength of him. Her palm pressed against his thudding heart, warming to the erratic rhythm. She sighed and her lips parted with his.

For a single heartbeat they were immobile. Time, the world, even their breaths, hung suspended in that one unending moment. Then, with a low, anguished moan, he repossessed her parted lips and this kiss was fierce and hot and acutely demanding.

Without even a token of resistance, Beth surrendered fully to his demand. Her body melted against his, so warm it burned right through her dress. Her hands wound into his hair, so soft it whispered through her fingers. Her whole being was absorbed by him, enthralled by his kiss.

Years of restraint gave way to a tumult of passion. With a shuddering groan he whisked his hands over her, over the smooth, supple skin of her bare back to the curve of her hips, slick and evasive in her dress. He'd fantasized about holding her, caressing her, but no fantasy had ever produced the creamy velvet of her skin, the fragrant silk of her hair, the gentle rise of her breasts with each breath she drew. He kissed her urgently, feverishly, thoroughly, and still could not get enough. No woman had ever tasted so sweet, felt so warm, filled him with such searing need.

Beth thrummed to the heated delirium of his kisses, wanting to dissolve within them. She wanted every fiber of her being to fuse with his. She wanted him. Consumed with wanting, she eagerly arched toward him, offering herself completely.

Her abrupt action caught him off guard and knocked him off balance. He toppled back, but managed to break his fall and right himself almost instantly. But it broke the keenly intense spell that had bound them. After a stunned second, both laughed. Full and rich, it brought them together as even their passion had not done. A bountiful exhilaration lifted Beth beyond her physical excitement. She felt intoxicated, lightheaded with happiness.

Somewhere in the midst of their impassioned captivation, twilight had given way to nightfall. The air had cooled and Beth shivered to feel its chill nip her skin. Kaler immediately drew her into the circle of his arm. She snuggled against his warmth contently, feeling secure and warmed in heart as much as body.

They sat companionably, enjoying the gradual display of stars. He pointed out the constellation called Orion. In turn, she indicated Cassiopeia's whereabouts. Softly telling her how often he had yearned to see the stars without bars or screens blocking his view, he nestled his lips into her hair.

She shivered again, this time from the yearning to take all his hurts unto herself, to give him an unlimited view of the stars for all time. His mouth felt warm and good within her hair. She peeked up at him. The emotions she saw cross his face left her breathless.

Never before had she seen him without his defensive mask in place. But now she saw vulnerability and fear and desire and, yes, love too.

"Kaler," she breathed.

His name was a soft endearment on her lips. Hearing it thrilled him. He had no words in him to tell her how much. "Ummm," he murmured, his breath caressing her hair.

"Do you still find me fatiguing?"

"You know I don't." He smiled tenderly.

"What then?" She blew the hint of a kiss over his mouth, but skittered away before he could claim the substance of it. "What do you find me?"

"Stimulating," he answered, "seductively stimulating."

She laughed, low and throaty, and Kaler could no longer keep from capturing his kiss. At first, he nibbled gently, parting her lips with his tongue and exploring with tantalizing leisure. She was warmly responsive, and gentleness swiftly simmered into ardent excitement.

His hands skimmed from her hip to her stomach to the swell of her breasts, where he lingered to savor the special resiliency. Her nipples stiffened, straining against the bodice of her dress. He wondered if her aureoles were brown or pink and whether she would like the feel of his tongue caressing them. He wondered whether she would like the feel of his body against hers, without anything in between to restrict them; whether she would like his body joining with hers, sharing the special joy of fulfillment.

He longed to tell her he loved her, tell her how good she felt, how much he ached for her. He wanted to reassure her that he'd never hurt her, that he wished only to take care of her. But those were the sorts of things he could never say to her. All that he could not say, he put into the fervent kisses he pressed upon her lips, her chin, her throat.

Each kiss swept Beth further into the vortex of her desires. She felt as if she'd been swept away by a tornado, swirling through a tempest of sensations. She no longer heard the chirruping night creatures symphonizing

150

around her; she heard only the rasping catch of their breaths, the thundering gallop of their hearts. The chill of the air no longer nipped her skin; her goose bumps rose solely from the tingling of her nerves to his touch. Her senses reeled and her body quivered and she returned each of his kisses with a tempestuous torrent of her own.

"I want you," she groaned on a husky note. "I want you and need you and want you."

The impassioned offer raged within his blood until he thought his veins would burst from the intensity. He wanted her so desperately, the pleasure he felt was painful. But a single thread of self-control remained unbroken. Grasping it, Kaler forced himself to pull back. Her face was a milky silhouette in the dark. He gulped in air.

"Beth," he whispered hoarsely. "Beth, we've got to—"

Fearing he would say what she did not want to hear, wanting this to go on and on and on into infinity, she set the tips of her fingers on his lips and sighed unsteadily, "We've got each other, and we've got the rest of the evening."

He kissed the pads of her fingers, then lifted her hand and tenderly kissed the center of her palm. With agonizing deliberateness he set her hand in her lap.

"We can't," he said, and there was a wealth of pain in his voice.

The heat surging through her slowly banked. She sat upright and fussed busily with her clothes, her hair. With a sinking heart she realized that her confession must have made a difference after all. His physical response had been obvious. She could only conclude he no longer wanted her because she no longer fit his image of her. She thought bitterly how right those women were who said you should never tell the man you love your past secrets. She'd felt guilty, having him think her so perfect, so saintly. She should have let him go on believing the lie. Instead, she'd knocked herself off her own pedestal.

"I guess I've disappointed you," she said stiffly.

Kaler inhaled deeply. Desire still clamored, pounding through his veins, throbbing within his loins. He heard her, but her words scarcely made sense to his drumming ears. "What?" he returned blankly.

"It's because of what I told you," she added, scorn and sadness mingled together.

It took several seconds for her meaning to get through to him. He couldn't believe she could think something so utterly stupid. His first response was a stupefied, "What?"

"It's because you think badly of me now that you know just how unsaintly I can be." She attempted a smile. Her mouth quivered. She sucked in her lower lip to stop its trembling. She wouldn't give him the satisfaction of her tears.

His second reaction was a strong suggestion that she get her brains unscrambled. "How in God's name could you ever think I'd think less of you—for any reason? I'm the last person in the world to judge others, but least of all, to judge you. Whatever happened, and I believe it was more his fault than yours, whatever happened doesn't dim you at all in my eyes. I know how good, how gentle, how—"

Her trembling lip slipped from between her teeth and with one warning sniff she began crying. "I disappointed you! I'm not what you thought I was. I'm so much less—"

Again, his arms came round her. Again, he comforted her with the warmth of his shoulder. He soothingly rubbed her back with his palm and again desire for her pulsated through him, demanding release. But this time his physical pangs were submerged in an upswell of tenderness, in a surge of longing to ease her emotional suffering more than his physical torment.

"I could never think badly of you, Beth, never. No

matter what you've done. You could've walked the streets of Minneapolis for a decade and it wouldn't change the admiration I feel for you."

"It must have changed something," she insisted. She sniffed back another large sob. "Otherwise, why don't you want me?"

"Don't want you?" He took her by the shoulders and held her away from him, staring at her as if she'd just confessed to being an undercover cop. "Don't want you?" he repeated, dumfounded.

She hung her head and sniffed.

"My God, don't you realize I'm throbbing with wanting you?" he asked. "I'm sore from wanting you. I've wanted you so much, for so long, that all it takes is a whiff of your perfume—no, not even that. Just the thought of you. Just picturing your smile or remembering your laughter and I get so worked up, I ache with wanting."

Raising her head, Beth gaped at him. There was no mistaking the truth in that vehement speech. "But what's wrong then? Why did you push me away?"

He ruffled his hair impatiently. "Because I can't let you get mixed up with me."

"But I want to be mixed up with you!" she cried in frustration.

"You don't understand what that means, Beth," he said, and though he'd meant it to be gentle, it came out mournfully harsh. "The looks, the talk—you had a taste of it tonight—"

"It was nothing!" she burst in.

"Yes," he conceded, "it was nothing. But think about enduring it all the time, every day, wherever you go, because you're with me or associated with me. People talk—"

"A little talk won't bother me."

"No matter how much you tell yourself you don't care,

153

you do," he corrected her grimly. "I know. I've suffered such talk all my life."

"I'm not made of porcelain, Kaler. I can handle it."

"You think that now because you don't fully realize what it can be like, being isolated from everyone else, being socially untouchable. You wouldn't be just Beth Rasmussen anymore, you'd be Beth Rasmussen, that O'Connell's woman. And that's if they were being kind."

She personally thought being considered O'Connell's woman would suit her to a T, but she wasn't quite sure how to tell him so. "What I'd be is with you," she equivocated. "That's the important thing, not what anyone else might say about me."

To be with her—it sounded like all the dreams that had filled years of cold, lonely nights melded together in one glorious design. But that was the problem. It was only a dream. It could never be more than that.

"I want you, Beth. I can't tell you how much I want you." He longed to stop there, but steeled himself to go on. "But I care enough to want what's best for you. I can't let you make a foolish mistake, and Lord knows, getting mixed up with me would be a mistake that went way past foolish."

"Who are you to say what I can or can't do?" she demanded. "If I want to make such a *mistake*"—she sneered the word—"how do you intend to stop me?"

"I'll find a way. I'll have to." He clasped his hands between his knees and stared down at them. "I'll have to keep you from throwing yourself into the mess I've made of my life. For your own good."

"Don't you start that! I'm sick and tired of everyone else knowing what's for my own good. Everyone thinks they can rule my life, *for my own good*, but I'm the only one who can say what's best for me. I'm the only one who knows what's in my heart." She reached for him, longing to hold him and show him what was in her heart.

Kaler jerked out of her reach. He knew if he let her touch him it would all be over. He'd grab her and the rest of the world be damned. But for her sake he fought his raging desires, and somehow he managed to slowly drawl, "Like you knew what was best for you in Minneapolis?"

Her lungs emptied on a sharp gust. Her arms fell to her sides. "We can all make mistakes," she said quietly. "You, of all people, should know that."

He came abruptly to his feet. "Where are you going?" she asked dully, not certain at the moment whether she really cared.

He pushed his hair back from his brow. It gentled into place and he sighed. "I need to walk a bit. I won't go far."

"Oh," she said, feeling frustrated and more than a little deflated. She watched his silhouette fade into the darkness behind the schoolhouse, then sat listening to the wind rustle the leaves amid the myriad hum of nightsongs. The sky was now a brilliantly deep blue, speckled with stars and striated with faint grayish wisps. She thought how ironic it was that when she finally made up her mind to love Kaler O'Connell, to brave all opposition, to face down all those who'd have her suppress her feelings for her own good, O'Connell the lady-killer should choose to be noble. *For her own good.*

It was these little ironies that sometimes made her feel that life was too complicated for her. At such times she couldn't even figure out what she felt, much less how to deal with it. She knew she was angry, bitterly angry at all those who'd ever made Kaler feel so unwanted and unworthy. She knew she was disappointed, deeply disappointed, and a shade embarrassed, too, at having her advances rejected by him. She knew she was depressed, pervasively depressed, at his insistence to keep her at arm's length. He could be more immutable than the Rock of Gibraltar once he set his mind to something.

"What do I do?" she sighed into the shadows. She waited breathlessly, but the night returned no answer. When she heard his footfall, she jumped up to meet him face to face. But she didn't meet his face, she met his mask, the detached, impenetrable mask that shielded his thoughts from the world.

"I want you to know," he began with a stiff formality that thoroughly snuffed any spark of hope she'd still carried, "that I do care for you, very much. I've valued your friendship more than I can tell you. But I made a mistake in encouraging you as I have. Besides alienating you from your family and friends—"

"That's not completely true. Only Dale has been such an ass and my true friends like me despite my . . ." She groped for the right phrase.

"Your lack of judgment?" he supplied.

She was glad it was too dark for him to see her flush. "Despite whether or not they agree with me a hundred percent, about anything," she amended.

He didn't think he could withstand much more of this. His soul was shattering and he feared that all too soon his control would shatter with it. He had to convince her to drop it and now.

"Our friendship has been . . . frustrating . . . for me," he said tonelessly. "For my good as much as for yours, I think we'd do best to call a halt to it."

This was worse, far worse, than anything she'd feared. She had never expected him to tell her it was over between them. Her mouth parted and her fingers flew up to hold back any cries that might try to escape. Finally she was able to say unsteadily, "You don't mean that."

"It's for the best."

His voice was without inflection, his expression completely blank. He was dead to any pleading or reasoning she might try to make. Beth slumped, then turned on her heel and returned to her car. He joined her and they drove off in wordless misery.

The night that had begun with such promise had ended with unbearable pain.

Muffling the closing of the screen door as much as she could, Beth removed her high-heeled sandals and crossed the kitchen on cat's feet. Adroitly maneuvering in a zig-zag to avoid the creakiest steps, she mounted the stair-case, then paused, listening tensely at the top. The house was blanketed in sleep. She snuck into the sanctuary of her room in relief.

She felt no older than Jenny, tiptoeing in after a too-late session of making out. She winced at the image. He'd said the old schoolhouse was where he'd taken all the girls to make out. He still did, she qualified gloomily. She wondered if he kept a scorecard, and just to add a bit of salt to her wound, figured she'd probably rated a zero.

She hurt. God how she hurt! She'd thought that Lance had left her immune to such gnawing pain. But this was much worse than anything she'd felt then. When Lance had rejected her, her misery had been mitigated by an underscoring relief. Deep down she'd been glad to get out of it. She felt no relief now. All she felt was pure unadulterated heartache.

Her dress slid to the floor in a crinkling hush. Un-characteristically, she let it lay, stepping over its folds to drop her underthings alongside it. She didn't even stop to don her baby-doll pajamas; she just slid beneath the floral-printed sheets and huddled in a tight ball, determined never to think of him again.

Naturally she thought of him. She pressed her cheek into her palm and thought of her last sight of him, out-side the Late-Nite Liquor Store. He'd insisted she leave him there rather than drive him home. Against all her resolutions not to, she protested. "But this isn't the best place for you to be seen!"

For her pains she received a defiant stare that curdled her blood. Her lower lip trembled dangerously. She stared out over the steering wheel, working hard not to make a fool of herself with a flood of tears. Her face always splotched when she cried. As light as a dandelion puff dancing on wind his fingertip glanced her cheek. She swiveled widened eyes to him.

The defiance had receded, replaced by a sorrowing to reflect her own. "Don't worry about me. It's not worth your time. I can take care of myself."

"Like you have in the past?" she shot back.

He drew in his lips, a bittersweet amusement shuttering his pain. "Tit for tat, Beth? Let me reassure you, I intend to take much better care of myself in the future. As soon as I've got enough money together, I'm going to leave here and start off new somewhere else. Just as soon as I can afford to do it," he reiterated as he reached for the door. When he got out, he hesitated. He looked back. "You'll take care of yourself, won't you?"

"Yes," she whispered through lips that barely parted.

"Be sure you do."

And he had stepped into the garish neon illumination beneath the liquor store sign. She'd driven off with her gaze straight ahead, but hadn't been able to keep from looking in the rearview mirror. Though her vision blurred, she'd clearly seen him entering the store.

So she coiled on her bed and wondered and worried. Was he out drinking? With whom? Would he end up back in prison? She worried until she shook with released sobs, then furiously demanded to know what the hell did she care anyway? She didn't give a darn about Kaler O'Connell and never had.

When she couldn't convince herself of that, she let the

158

tears fall, soaking her pillow and saturating her grieving soul.

The first thing he became aware of was the spinning. The bed was spinning viciously. He opened his eyes. Not the bed. The room. He closed his eyes and groaned. It didn't help. He lay very still and prayed for a quick and merciful death.

Later, he woke a second time and discovered that though the bed and the room had stopped spinning, his stomach had taken up the slack. It heaved violently. He scrambled up and down the hall to the bathroom he shared with four other boarders. It was fortunately unoccupied and he emptied his stomach of its severe distress.

Still later, as he dressed with shaking hands, he struggled to remember where he had gotten drunk and with whom. His last clear memory was of Beth's profile, frozen into remote dispassion, as she pulled out of a parking lot.

What parking lot? he wondered and groped around for his shoes. He knocked into a bottle and sent it spinning. A clear liquid sloshed wildly in the bottom. It reminded him too vividly of his stomach and he shut his eyes again.

And then he remembered.

He remembered the wonderful evening, the beauty of the night enhanced by the beauty of Beth. He remembered the feel of her, the creamy texture of her skin, the silken softness of her hair. He remembered the perfumed scent that grew stronger with her ardor and the passionate fervor that heightened with each kiss. He remembered and he felt himself warming with the memories.

He opened his eyes and slowly bent to pick up the tequila bottle. He remembered, then, which parking lot. The end of the evening had been the end of his dreams. He had done what he had to do, for her sake, but it had cost him dearly. It would be so much more lonely going on without her now than it would have been had he never met her.

A spurt of rage shook him. How he wished he'd never met her! How he wished he'd never come back to Pasque! It had been a mistake, another damned act of pride that had ultimately backfired on him. Hadn't he learned by now he didn't have to prove anything to anyone else? He only had to prove himself to himself.

So what had he proved? He'd proved he could still drink like an idiot. He straightened, then weaved back to the bathroom, where he poured the contents of the bottle down the drain, then tossed it into the wastebasket beneath the sink. For all the good it would do him, he'd at least had the sense to bring the bottle back to his room and drink alone. At least he'd stayed away from more trouble, even if he hadn't achieved anything more worthwhile than a wrenching hangover. He'd also proved that he couldn't drown his misery in alcohol. This was the unsinkable kind of misery, the kind you had to learn to live with, day in and day out.

Back in his room, he stretched down on his bed, which to his relief remained motionless, and offered up a prayer of thanks that he had the day to sober up. Not that he could keep his drunken night a secret. Nothing was ever kept secret in Pasque. By now half the town probably knew he'd bought a bottle of tequila last night, and was busily enlightening the other half. He wondered if it meant he could expect an unscheduled visit from his parole officer. How he yearned to get away from it all, from the restrictions and the gossip.

He remembered telling Beth he intended to leave town and start fresh somewhere else. It would be, he knew, the best thing. The farther he got from Beth, the better. Maybe the misery that liquor couldn't blot would fade with distance.

But he needed money to start somewhere new, and

160

though he lived frugally, he hadn't saved enough. He was stuck in Pasque, stuck with the continual reminders of Beth and the aching and the wanting and the loneliness. If he just had the money, he'd get away from it all.

CHAPTER TWELVE

An uneasy anticipation hung like a guillotine blade, finely honed and sharpened, waiting only for the right moment to drop. Everyone seemed to feel its hovering edge. Lisa unreasonably snapped at Dee within fives minutes of arriving at work and the two fumed in antagonistic silence thereafter. Janet spilled coffee over a stack of letters she'd just finished typing and snarled if anyone so much as glanced at her. Leonard slammed himself into his office to again review the month's inventory and audit, which no matter how often he reworked it was not computing as it should have. Even Nelda was unusually sharp as she directed Beth to proof the Christmas catalogues before they were sent on to the printer.

It briefly occurred to Beth to point out that as she hoped she knew her job, she'd very naturally already proofed the catalogues, but her apathy won out over her annoyance. She really couldn't get worked up enough to defend herself. She simply didn't care, not about her job, not about her life. It was more than a week after her evening with Kaler, and she still couldn't find an interest in anything.

"Yes, Nelda," she said listlessly.

Nelda's head bounced up. "My God, not you too. I can't stand it."

"Stand what?" asked Beth, her tone heavy with indifference.

"This widespread attack of Monday-morning blahs."

Beth shrugged.

Nelda forcibly shoved her pencil into her hair, where it completely disappeared within the tight gray curls. Her old wooden swivel chair creaked as she leaned back, bent an elbow on the arm, and propped her chin on it. "I was counting on you, Beth, to be the ray of sunshine amidst all the gloom and doom, and here you are, meekly yessing me when I know perfectly well you must have gone over those catalogues at least once already."

Beth acknowledged this with a lethargic bob of her head.

Gnashing her teeth hadn't been the same since she'd gotten her dentures, so Nelda eschewed this pleasure and dismissed her employee, muttering, "Don't come near me until Tuesday. Don't let anyone else near me either. I can't stand Mondays like this."

It was amazing how her feet could be moving one after the other, carrying her back to her office, when her body felt like deadweight. Beth concentrated on this astounding accomplishment, watching each step her feet made. It took effort, but by dint of focusing her thoughts on her amazing feet, she was able, for a moment, to elude the continual houndings of her "what ifs."

What if she refused to give in? What if she went to him and told him outright that she loved him? What if she told him she wasn't going to give up without a fight? What if she dogged his heels the way thoughts of him dogged her?

Feet. She should be thinking about her poor feet, having to haul around this sluggish, uncooperative body. She looked down past her dull gray skirt to her sensible black pumps, sensibly taking her to her office, and came to a

163

crashing halt as she smashed head-on into a masculine chest.

Gold and silver lacings showered over her. A box hit the floor with a thumping plop and a highly descriptive expletive reverberated in the air.

"Sorry," Eddie Curran grumbled as he righted himself. He didn't sound sorry at all; he sounded disgusted. He looked even more so as he inspected the array of trims littering the floor.

"I'm the sorry one," Beth said. "I wasn't looking where I was going."

He gave her a glance that clearly said, why the hell not? But he said nothing. Bending, he began scooping handfuls of the trims into the box. Beth plucked a few off the shoulders of her pleated Victorian blouse, then stooped and helped him retrieve the rest. When she handed him the last gold lacing, she again apologized.

"Forget it," he growled, sounding as if he would remember it until his dying day.

"Well, uh, tell Lisa I—"

"Don't," he interrupted brusquely, "mention Lisa Ingram to me. Not today, not ever."

He snatched the lacing from her hand and stomped on down the corridor. Beth gaped at his back until he disappeared around the first corner. Great, she thought with a mental sigh. On top of everything else, an office lovers' spat.

Must be the wrong time of year for lovers, she thought dolefully. Romance is in the end-of-summer slump. Maybe if she waited until spring, Kaler's fancy might be more compliant. She thought of spring, of the joyful rejuvenation, the planting and birthings at the farm, the blossoming flowers and budding trees, and she spun a daydream of sprinkling wild flower petals over his glossy, fine hair, of raining a kiss for every petal. . . .

Another sigh, this one glumly audible, accompanied

her into the refuge of her own office. She ought to know better than to permit such dreams to enter her head. Dreams led to disappointments and she'd had enough disappointments in this lifetime.

She sank into her chair to wait, then realized she had no idea what she was waiting for. Shaking herself, she gathered together the catalogue galleys and decided to check them one more time before sending them off to the printer.

If polled, not a single employee at Creative Crafts would have thought the afternoon could possibly be worse than that Monday morning. If so polled, every employee would have been wrong. Directly after lunch a minor accident at the dock sent two of Dutch's loaders home for the day, shifting an extra burden onto everyone else, and one of his pickers up and quit without notice. Dutch ranted to Nelda, who in turn demanded to know why Leonard had not yet given her the month-end balance sheet.

"Because," he explained icily, "I haven't balanced it yet."

"So get it balanced," ordered Nelda, and both stormed back to their respective offices.

An hour later Leonard charged into Nelda's office and pitched an accounting sheet on the center of her desk. Ignoring Beth's presence, he stabbed a long finger at a column of computerized figures. "There," he said triumphantly. "Right there."

Nelda painstakingly lifted his finger and removed it from her sight before perusing the itemized figures. Beth locked her fingers together and studied them, trying to recount precisely how many days, weeks, months, it had taken her to stop pining for Lance. She estimated, then doubled, tripled the figure. That was her estimate for how long her heart would grieve for Kaler.

165

"What's where?" Nelda finally asked of Leonard.

He tapped an impatient foot to underscore his annoyance with her apparent dullness. "There. The imbalance." He leaned forward and indicated a credit figure.

"So?" she said, looking up at him.

"So it doesn't correspond with the deposit receipts." He spread another sheet in front of her. He indicated a difference of slightly over two hundred dollars in the total amount.

Standing beside her employer, Beth couldn't help but see the figures. She sidled around the desk. "Perhaps I should leave you two," she murmured to her inattentive audience.

"Checking the ledger item by item against the ladings," continued Leonard, "I discovered this." With a flourish he produced a thin blue paper. A square of smeary red ink read PAID IN FULL. Beneath that, handwritten in, was CASH. The amount corresponded to the penny with the figure on the accounting sheet. It was slightly over two hundred more than the sum of the bank deposits.

Inching toward the door, Beth again said, "I'll just be going. . . ."

"Hold on a minute," commanded Nelda. "I think you may need to know what this is about." She gestured imperiously and Beth had no choice but to return. She didn't care to know what it was about; she didn't care about anything. Didn't anyone understand that?

Nelda took the lading in hand and examined it thoroughly. It was dated exactly a week earlier, the previous Monday. "Another Monday mess," she huffed under her breath. "I assume, Leonard, that you've told no one else about this discrepancy."

The statement was in actuality a question, and Leonard promptly assured her that he'd told no one. He gazed down his long nose at her and said snippily, "I naturally

166

wished to call it to your attention before drawing any conclusions."

It was obvious, however, that he had drawn a conclusion, the only conclusion that seemed logical. No one uttered the word, but Beth knew they were all thinking it.

"Naturally," cooed Nelda, soothing his offended sensibilities. "Please continue to keep this matter to yourself for the time being. I intend to make a thorough inquiry."

"Of course." With a brisk nod at them both, Leonard made his victorious exit.

Harmonizing with the click of the door, Nelda heaved a melancholy sigh. "He'll expect a raise for this," she said.

When Beth remained silent, Nelda glanced at her sharply. A string of restless nights had left Beth wan and lethargic, drained of her usual rosy complexion. Patting the chair beside her desk, Nelda told her to sit down. "Whatever it is that's bothering you, Beth, will just have to be shelved for the time being. I'd like to help you, but this will have to come first. We can't let a possible embezzlement wait for anything."

Though she'd spoken kindly, her speech was lashed with enough of a sting to prick Beth out of her mood. "Thank you, Nelda, but I'll cope. As you say, this matter must come first." A disquieting chill snaked up her spine. "Do you really think it could be . . . embezzlement?"

"I don't know. The entries in the ledger are taken from the ladings, so the first thing, I suppose, is to find out who accepted payment on this shipment last Monday and how much was actually received. Then we'll need to determine which of the girls made the bank deposit that day. I'll give you the easy one. You check this out." She waved the blue lading at Beth, who took it and stood.

"I'll get right on it."

"Be as discreet as you can—even though I know this'll be all over the plant in a matter of minutes," Nelda said

167

gloomily. As Beth went out she could clearly hear Nelda moaning. "I can't stand it, I can't stand another Monday like this."

All paperwork was coded; each employee marked what he or she handled with a special number. Although she recognized a few of the codes, mostly those of longtime employees, Beth didn't know very many of them. This was one she didn't recognize, so the first place she went was Dutch's office. As she walked through the warehouse her eyes explored the aisles, but did not find him. She wasn't certain whether she was disappointed or relieved.

She found Dutch at his desk, barking into the phone, "Hell, I'm sorry, but with two of my men out, I'm backlogged here. All I can tell you is that they'll get out as soon as I can get 'em out to you."

While he continued his conversation she tried not to survey anything beyond the glass overlooking the warehouse. She failed miserably. Her gaze continually flicked, searching, seeking, and, at last, finding. He strode down a row, coming closer and closer. Her heart lurched painfully. Then he turned abruptly and disappeared from view. It was just a glimpse, but it hurt. After nine days it surprised her that the wound could feel so agonizingly fresh.

"What can I do for you?" asked Dutch, sounding harried.

Jolted out of her misery, she handed him the lading bill. "Can you tell me who received the payment on this? I can't keep up with all the codes."

He glanced at it, then at her, narrowly. "Is there a problem I should know about?"

"We don't know yet," she replied. "I'd like to speak with whoever handled this."

"Today? We're pretty rushed today, what with the—"

"Today," she broke in firmly. "It's important."

After a long pause he grabbed his intercom microphone and intoned, "O'Connell, I need to see you for a minute."

The hair on the back of her neck stood on end. She stared stupidly at Dutch and moved her mouth soundlessly. Kaler!

The blade had dropped.

He stopped at the door of Dutch's cubicle. His eyes flashed silver as he saw her, but quickly dulled to a lusterless lead. Dutch excused himself and Beth had to restrain herself from flinging herself on him, wildly begging him to stay. She looked down, around, anywhere but at Kaler. It didn't matter whether she looked at him or not. He was the only object in the room. Her nerves thrummed with awareness of him.

Finally he said, "You wanted to see me about something?"

Caution muted his tone. She darted a look and saw that he held himself warily, alert for trouble. Hating having to do this, she gave him the bill. "Did you accept this payment?"

He didn't even glance at it. "You must know I did or you would be asking somebody else."

"Please, Kaler, don't make this any more difficult for me than it already is."

Her distress was real. He softened. After checking the lading, he handed it back to her. "Yes, I received it. Last Monday."

She riveted her eyes to the figure written on the bill. Swallowing hard, she wished she didn't have to ask him anything else. But she did. "Did—did you actually receive the full amount?"

The silence battered at her until she had to give up and look at him. He met her gaze with an empty stare. She balanced on the precipice of anguished doubt a few seconds longer, then crumpled the bill in her fist and fled.

At the back of her mind she was dimly aware that several people had observed the exchange through the glass windows, but she couldn't react to that now. She was too busy reacting to all the ugly suspicion and piercing doubt that mauled her. Her heart, her soul, her very being, rejected even the remotest suggestion that Kaler could have taken that money. But like the snake in the Garden of Eden, her mind twisted her faith. He'd told her, hadn't he, that all he needed was money to get out of town. It would have been so easy to pocket the cash. . . .

No! She fiercely repelled such a shameful supposition. He couldn't, he wouldn't. She returned to her office, determined to believe it.

Within the hour, the rumor blazed through the company. Money—some said as much as two thousand—was missing, and O'Connell had been questioned about it.

Beth couldn't bear the rash of accusatory whispers that erupted all around her. She hid in the ladies' room and was there when Lisa burst in, tearfully denying any wrongdoing. "All I did was take the packet and deposit slip to the bank! Leonard added up the deposit! *He's* the one, not me!"

The door swung open and Lisa angrily swiped her hands over her cheeks before facing Dee and Janet. "And you two just better not say anything to me ever again. The way you looked at me as if . . . as if I were a crook or something!"

"We didn't mean anything like that, Lisa honey," soothed Janet. "We know you're nothing of the kind."

"Besides," put in Dee, "we all know who's really guilty."

Beth's hackles rose instantly. She rounded on the trio and demanded coldly, "Just what do you mean by that?"

"Well, surely, you can't believe—" sputtered Dee.

"I'll tell you what I believe. I believe you're spreading

170

a vicious rumor without just cause. We haven't even determined that anything other than an honest mistake has taken place. Without a crime, I don't see how anyone can be considered guilty."

"Leonard told us that it was as open and shut a case as he'd ever seen." Dee's plump face reddened with indignation.

"And Eddie says you've already questioned O'Connell about it," sniffed Lisa. "So why try to defend him?"

"We all knew when you hired him, you were making a mistake," Janet stated on a righteous note that made Beth's palm itch to slap her. Instead, giving them all one furiously withering look, she stalked out.

She went directly to Nelda's, entering without bothering to knock and raging, "Nelda, something's got to be done."

"I think I'm going to cut every Monday out of my calendar," grumbled Nelda without looking up. "What on earth can it be now?"

"Leonard has accused Kaler of taking the money and even said it was an open and shut case."

Real consternation sobered Nelda's grandmotherly features. Saying she'd better have a talk with him, she rose from her chair and together she and Beth went to find him. On the way, Beth explained all that she'd learned in the ladies' room. "Everyone just assumes he's guilty," she went on, "without even giving him a chance."

"It's true we can't make such baseless assumptions about him," agreed Nelda. "But, Beth, neither can we blindly assume he is not guilty."

The words rang like a death knell. They tolled so loudly in Beth's heart, she did not even derive the least satisfaction from hearing Nelda inform Leonard soundly that if he expressed one more opinion, just one, about what may or may not have been done by whom, it would mean his job.

171

"Not even a syllable," Nelda ordered with rare anger.

For once Leonard gave the appearance of sincerely apologizing. But Beth hardly noticed. The what-ifs had returned to haunt her. What if he'd really done it? What if he'd taken the money to get away from her? What if he had planned it all along? What if? Her fear escalated with each what-if that persecuted her.

She trailed Nelda into Dutch's office with a desolate heart. This was the worst nightmare she'd ever lived, far worse than the awful day she'd learned Lance was married, far, far worse than the day she'd realized he'd just been using her. This was worse than any nightmare. Nightmares end. This was going on and on until she thought she would scream.

Dutch and Kaler awaited them. Even as they entered, Dutch spoke up. "I want to go on record as saying I've got complete faith in O'Connell's job performance. I've let every worker in my warehouse know how I feel, and I'm ready to say the same to anyone else."

"That's high praise, coming from you," said Nelda mildly. Though remaining silent, Beth wanted to throw the foreman a wreath of roses. Someone, at least, supported her belief that Kaler must be innocent.

Nelda offered Kaler her hand. After a perceptible delay, he took it. "I want to apologize to you," she said in her direct way. "I sincerely regret the unfounded accusations to which you've been subjected. But the sooner we can get to the bottom of this, the sooner we'll have the rumors cleared out and dumped in the trash bin where they belong."

In her heart Beth begged Kaler not to use a sarcastic tone, not to be coldly defiant. *They don't know you as I do,* she silently whispered. *They won't understand that underneath you're scared and unhappy.*

"I'll do whatever is necessary," Kaler was saying, "to help you find out what happened."

172

"I appreciate your cooperation," Nelda said. "And your understanding."

"It's only natural you'd talk to me—I was the last to handle that particular shipment," he pointed out reasonably.

With a brisk nod Nelda got down to business and began grilling him on the receipt of the lading. Beth stared in wide-eyed admiration. Despite his tensed stance, despite his closed expression, his replies remained the epitome of reasoned calm. How difficult it must be for him, she could only guess, but she knew his restraint couldn't come easily. Her heart swelled with pride . . . and love.

Unexpectedly he looked her way. For a heartbreaking instant, the guard slipped. His gray eyes clouded with pain and longing and uncertainty. Her own eyes blurred with tears, she lifted a hand toward him and the shutter closed. He withdrew into his impenetrable shell. When Nelda dismissed him he didn't even glance Beth's way. He simply pivoted and strode out.

Five o'clock crawled in at long last. Beth felt as if she'd been through every emotion known to humankind, with a few extras thrown in for experimentation. Nelda's assurances that they'd get the matter settled as quickly as possible hadn't encouraged Beth in the least. Part of her feared the solution. As much as she wanted to believe otherwise, a nasty, nagging suspicion that maybe he had taken the money would not be stilled. She felt she would never be sure until she heard it from his own lips, until he told her, "I did not do it."

On impulse, she made a U-turn at one end of Main and headed back the other direction, past the train tracks and into the section of town where the houses looked as old as time. She had no very clear notion about what she meant to do, she only knew that she could not let a night pass by without some understanding between them. Nine days

173

of wordless pretense had been bad enough. This new barrier was unendurable.

In a narrow hall, facing the door with her knuckles raised, Beth had a major doubt. She almost turned tail and ran. What could she say? He wouldn't welcome her interference and she knew she couldn't stand any more of that indifference he put on. But one thing kept her from leaving.

Love. If anything, she loved him more than ever. Every protective instinct she possessed rushed to the fore. She wasn't going to let him go through this alone. Whatever he may have done, she was going to help him through it. Whether he wanted her or not, he needed her and she loved him too much to turn away.

She knocked. Closing her eyes, she took in as many deep breaths as she could.

The door wrenched open. "What are you doing here?" he asked.

She opened her eyes. He was still wearing his blue workshirt and jeans, his hair was charmingly mussed, his face uncharmingly remote.

"That's not a very friendly welcome," she said shakily.

"I'm not feeling very friendly."

"Please, Kaler, I just want to talk."

He held the door, as if ready to slam it in her face. She wondered if she'd have to climb through his window. With a brusque movement he suddenly stepped back and flung open the door. "Suit yourself," he said.

The room was small and spare, with a bare floor, a cracked ceiling, and a split shade in a curtainless window. The windowsill served as a bookshelf; still more books tumbled over the top of a chest of drawers, a corner desk, and a ladder-backed chair. To Beth, it looked depressingly Spartan.

"It's larger and cleaner than any cell," he said abruptly.

She spun around to face him. His eyes were like ashes, cold and gray. Her heart thudded sickeningly.

They were so different, so completely different. He was so dark and defensive, she so fair and vulnerably open. He distrusted love, happiness, all the things he'd never known. She had faith in the certainty of life's blessings. Would she be able to bridge those differences? It would take effort, a lot of effort. Did she even want to try?

Kaler jerked away, breaking the invisible lock that had held them together. He crossed to the window, set his hands on the frame, and contemplated the street. Her heart pounding, she waited. He wheeled around. "Well, aren't you going to ask me if I did it? Isn't that why you came?"

All the conviction she didn't have surged into her voice. "No. I don't have to ask. I know you didn't."

He stared at her for so long she thought she might faint from the sickening apprehension building in her. Then he extended his hand. Without hesitation she rushed to take it.

175

CHAPTER THIRTEEN

His fingers curled over her palm. He gazed into her eyes and saw within the blue depths what he'd so often yearned to see—love. Soft, glowing, acquiescent love. He bent his lips to her hand and whispered a kiss into its warm center.

"Loving me won't be easy," he warned.

"Love is never easy, not the lasting kind of love."

He set his lips against the pulse point of her wrist, feeling it beat frenetically for him. She played lightly with the ends of his hair. He lifted his head, their eyes met, and for an exquisite eternity neither dared move.

Then the pain of denial would no longer be borne. Kaler lifted her into his arms and carried her to his bed. Its lumpy springs squeaked as he settled their weight on it. Beth scarcely noted the lumps, the squeaks, the stark surroundings. She was aware only of him, of his breath misting her neck, of his mouth tenderly warming her throat, of his body squeezed next to hers.

He touched her slowly, questioningly, not quite able to believe that she was real. He'd had so many fantasies, so many frustrations. He feared he'd blink and she'd be gone. But this was no fantasy. She was real and warm and overwhelmingly exciting.

In his fantasies he'd been a terrific lover, wildly satisfying all the nameless, faceless women of the lost years.

More recently, his dreams had been of Beth, but her reaction had been the same: for her he'd been the perfect lover. But this was not a dream. She lay beside him, her breath mingling with his, and he knew he might not be the perfect lover. As out of practice as he was, he might not be much of a lover at all.

Exploring the delicate bone of her jaw, caressing the heated pulsing of her throat, he tried to quell the fear rising alongside his need. She wound her arms around him and sighed softly in his ear. He hesitated, then swept his palm downward to the sensitive peak of her breast. His fingers searched through the pleats of the crepe of her blouse, down to her stomach and back, but he could find no buttons. His fear that he might not satisfy her grew. He couldn't even find the damn buttons!

Lost in the rippling pleasure of that palm gliding over her breasts, those fingertips wandering through her pleats, Beth didn't at first realize what he was doing. But pressed as she was against him, she could feel the change in the tension of his muscles, and she slowly comprehended his problem. She caught his hand and slid it beneath her. Pressing a kiss onto his chin, she whispered, "They're in the back."

"It's been a long time," he said unsteadily.

"Forever," she agreed. "I've waited for you forever."

Her slender back warmed his palm, a pearl button cooled his fingertip. He gazed down at her face, softened with love for him, and his panic grew. "Too long," he grated, "it's been too long, Beth. I can't—"

She hushed his pain with a tender kiss. Her being flooded with a love such as she'd never before known, a love more radiant in the giving than in the receiving. She stroked the strong line of his jaw and let him see the radiance of her love.

"We'll go slowly," she said gently, "slowly into the night."

Her compassion, her understanding, undid him. In a voice raw with emotion, he cried, "Beth, Beth, I need you."

She wrapped him within the comfort of her arms. His tremors shook them both. "I know, I know," she crooned, "I need you too, Kaler. I need you and I love you."

"All my life I've needed you," he said into her shoulder. "Years and years of needing and wishing—"

"Shhh, shhh, I'm here now," she soothed him. "Now and always."

He raised his head to look at her with an intensity that left her dizzy. "All those wishes—I never dreamed they could be fulfilled so completely. I never dared dream of a woman like you. You're my every dream, Beth."

A crackling current electrified the air between them. With an intense charge all hesitations and doubts melted away. They swayed together. The bed creaked in uneven protest as they toppled over.

After waiting so long, the explosion of their passion violently consumed them. They kissed deliriously. They touched with frenzied ardor. They came to know each other eagerly, impatiently. At some point Beth slid his shirt from his shoulders, kissing his chest down to his stomach as she did. And then he kissed the length of her spine, button by button as the crepe blouse fell away from her body. The rest of their clothing came off in bits and pieces, between caresses that sent them soaring and kisses that spiraled deeper, deeper, carrying them further into the world of sensation.

Though his palms were callused, his touch was so ethereal, Beth remembered only the delicacy of his rousing strokes. She lingered over her own exploration of him, savoring the firm muscles, relishing the flexure of them. His skin was smooth and warm; in places it was so heated he seemed to scorch her fingertips.

178

Kaler could not believe the wonder of her. The resilient softness of her breast filled his palm, the responsive buds stiffened to his gentle massage. The plane of her stomach was downy and pliant; her thighs were silk and satin. Her lightest touch took him to heaven; her every kiss was paradise.

It seemed to him he had waited a dozen lifetimes for her. As he raised his hips above hers, as he fused his being with hers, he vowed to love her for the next dozen.

He bent his head into the arch of her neck and hoarsely sighed her name as he made her his. She felt warm and wet and so utterly exquisite he had to strain to hold himself back. Slow, sweet strokes gradually became harder, faster, more imperative.

As his heated breath nuzzled her throat and he filled her with his hard warmth, Beth filled with the joy of being a woman, of being *his* woman. She softly cried his name again and again, a pledge to him that she was his, in every way possible.

The narrow bed shrieked ever more loudly. Kaler's breath rasped hot against her skin. Beth pressed her fingers into his back and she clung to the sweat-dampened muscles as they shifted with each thrust of pleasure.

Lifting his head, Kaler saw the satisfaction, the ultimate delight cross her face. The beauty of her passion took him over the edge. His body tightened and he gasped. Her body clenched with the tremors of mutual rapture. Gradually they rhythmically slowed to stillness. They twined together, sated in body, bound in soul, quietly drinking in the glory of it.

His breath returned and his heart steadied. He gently stroked the silk of her hair, working up the courage to say to her what he'd never said to anyone in his life. At length he whispered, "I love you, Beth. I always will."

"And I, you," she said with hushed happiness. She played her fingertip on the lobe of his ear, then blew once, lightly, over it. "I realized I loved you the day you gave me *The Prophet,* but I never knew how much until now."

He was aglow in the rapture that only secure love can bring. He felt lazily replete. "How much is that?" he drawled.

She pinched her fingers together. " 'Bout this much."

He playfully swatted her rear end, then made up for it by kissing her breathless. With his kiss his own hunger renewed itself. He didn't think he could ever get enough of her.

"I'll take what I can get," he said when he finally broke away, "and I'll give it back to you, Beth. I'll give anything to please you. I've missed you so much. This week was hell."

"I was miserable," she agreed. "I was so depressed, no one could stand being around me. Jenny told me I was acting worse than Joan Crawford in *Mommie Dearest.*"

He traced the line of her cheek with his fingertip. "My pride's always been my downfall, the fate of the Irish, I guess, but you always knew just how to get through my armor. I think that's why I first started to love you; you knew how to melt my foolish pride. You believe in me more than I believe in myself. Like coming here tonight, trusting in me."

She hoped he'd think her suddenly jumping pulse stemmed from his swirling caress. She must never, never let him know she'd doubted him, not even for a second. And truly, deep down in her heart, she hadn't doubted him at all. Her heart had led her straight to him.

Her mouth softened in a loving smile. "I always did believe in you, right from the first. I was defending you even before you came to Crafts for a job."

"I thought then it was just your kind heart, that you were feeling sorry for me. I resented it. I thought I resented it because I didn't want to be anybody's charity

180

case, but the real reason was that I wanted your love, not your pity."

"Even then? You wanted my love even back then?"

"Well," he drawled with a rakish smile, "I certainly wanted your sexy little body."

She stuck her tongue out at him, then flicked it lightly over his lips. "You got it," she breathed. "You got it all."

He wanted to ask, for how long? But he didn't want to press her; he didn't want her to shy away because he was too demanding. So he told her it was about time and kissed her soundly.

They lay, not speaking, comforting each other with gentling strokes and occasional light kisses. Kaler was wrapped within the bliss of it. This would be the moment he would treasure for the rest of his life, this tranquil, tender moment with Beth. Her special serenity gave him true contentment.

Her serenity was slightly ruffled, however, as Beth fished around for a delicate way to ask him what his intentions were. It was too soon. If she pressed him too hard, he might decide he didn't love her that much after all. Drawing curlicues on his chest with her fingertip, she inquired offhandedly, "Kaler, did you ever have any girlfriends? Anyone you cared about?"

"Jealous?" he countered, looking pleased. He scooped up her fingertip and nibbled on it. "Remember Vikki Johannsen? She stuck by me when I first went in, but it didn't last long. I didn't expect it to."

Beth remembered Vikki only vaguely. She'd been one of *those* girls, one who was spoken about in whispers. Had he loved her? A little stab of jealousy pricked her. "Why didn't you expect it to last?"

"That's the way it is when you're in prison. People on the outside tend to forget you when you're on the inside. Out of sight, out of mind."

He said it so matter-of-factly that it pierced her and she exclaimed fiercely, "I wouldn't forget you!"

"And that's why I love you," he murmured. He distracted her for a time with several well-placed kisses, but Beth wasn't to be sidetracked for long. She wanted to find out what he'd felt, what he might still feel for his long-ago love.

"So what happened exactly?"

He shrugged. "She just visited less and less frequently and then one day she didn't show at all. I called and she said she'd explain next time, but there wasn't ever a next time. I didn't blame her. It's too much trouble to go through all the security checks, the questions, the waiting, just to visit some con. It pales after a while."

"Were you sorry? Did you love her?" Beth pressed.

"You know what I'm going to do with you?" he asked.

She shook her head on the pillow.

"I'm going to send you to law school. You can become the state D.A. and bring home piles of money."

She balled her fist and punched his stomach. He retaliated by pressing her backward and muffling all her shrieks with a smothering kiss. She kicked vainly; he wrapped his legs over hers. Already, he was aroused, the loveplay would have turned serious if someone hadn't pounded on his door.

They both shot up, gaping first at the door then at each other. "Oh, my God," said Kaler, and he scrambled off the bed to toss her a lacy bra, a frilled half-slip, satin ice-blue undies.

"What are you doing?" she asked as this rainbow of lingerie splayed over her.

Another fervent knock reverberated through the small room.

"Get dressed," ordered Kaler. He yanked on his blue jeans and ran up the zipper. His head went to the left then the right, he scooped up her blouse and yelled, "I'm coming," then tossed the blouse to her.

Beth folded her hands in her lap and watched him.

"My God, aren't you dressed yet?" he asked. He looked around wildly. "The closet isn't very big, but if you're quiet—"

"Kaler, I don't care," she said.

The hammering at the door became insistent. Kaler threw open the closet and began pushing her clothes into it. "Come on, hurry up, if you're seen here, everyone'll know—"

"I don't care if I'm seen," she said with emphasis.

He stopped shoving clothes into the closet and stared at her. Beth had never looked more like her mother, with the possible exception of a lack of clothing. "You don't care?" he echoed.

"Not if you plan to make an honest woman of me."

To the repeated banging on his door Kaler addressed a mild curse and an order to wait a minute. To the naked woman with the tender half smile sitting on his bed, he issued a demand to know what she was talking about.

"It's leap year," she said, "and I just asked you to marry me."

He stared, he gaped, he considered having his hearing tested. He'd probably have stood like stone for the rest of his life if the pounding on the door hadn't shaken him. He flung up his hands. "I accept. Now for God's sake, put something on. As lovely as I think your birthday suit is, I don't think anyone we know could stand the shock of seeing you in it."

"Thanks a lot," she said, laughing lightly as she slid out of the bed. She grabbed his workshirt and went to stand behind him as she worked the buttons.

Her slight shadow warmed his back. Kaler set his hand on the knob and hoped with all his heart it wasn't a policeman or a parole officer who'd come in connection

183

with the problem at Crafts. Once Beth realized all the hassles that were a part of his life, she might take back her offer of marriage, and though he felt obligated to point out all the problems and reasons against it, the one thing he wanted most in this life was to marry her. With suspicion and dread he at last pulled open the door.

"It's about time. We were beginning to think you'd stashed a—" Nelda stopped dead in her tracks a foot over the threshold. Her brows rose as she took in the sight of her half-dressed employees standing together.

"Hi, Nelda," said Beth, waving a floppy sleeve at her from behind Kaler's back. "Kaler and I are getting married."

"Beth, we only—"

"Hi, Dutch," she said, ignoring Kaler's attempt to speak. "Did you hear the news?"

"May I offer you my congratulations?" Like the innate gentleman he was, Dutch averted his eyes from Beth, looking more toward the peeling patch in the wall beside her.

"Gracious, Beth, you rip through news like a tornado," declared Nelda. "I'm knocked flatter than Elmer Jackson's barn."

No one had been flattened flatter than Kaler. He hadn't expected her to tell anyone, much less to announce it so openly, so happily, so proudly. With difficulty he gathered himself together and said, "Hello, Mrs. Evenson."

"Call me Nelda. I don't stand on ceremony. All those formalities get in the way of all the really important things." She ran an eye over Beth. "I guess there's no need to ask if you're happy. You're disgustingly bright with it."

"Glowing from top to toe," Beth chirped.

Reaching out, Nelda searched for Beth's hand, lost in

the blue sleeve, and gave it a loving squeeze. "You'd better be good to her, young man, or you'll answer to me."

The women laughed. Kaler watched Beth shine and he softened. For her sake he would learn to accept these commonplace remarks without thinking they held a challenge for him. Dutch waited stoically for the laughter to die away, then cleared his throat. "Perhaps we should get on with business, Nelda, and then leave the two young ones alone."

"You're right as you almost always are, Dutch. We came to tell you, Kaler, that today's problem has been cleared up. There never was any missing money. The day that deposit was made, last Monday, was also the day I left for Fargo, remember, Beth? It was a one-day trip, I knew I wouldn't need much in the way of money, so I raided the cash we'd received that day. At the time I made a note of the debit, but somewhere in my rush to get on my way, the note got lost. In the tempest of the morning no one had a clear enough head to think of it."

"You're sure?" said Beth quietly.

"I found the note myself in my checkbook when I went to the grocery store. I called Dutch and we came right over here."

"I want you to know, Kaler, that even if Nelda hadn't found her note, I wanted you to stay on in the warehouse. You work hard and you do good work." Dutch put out his hand.

Kaler took it. For the first time in his life he felt like an equal. He glanced at Beth. With Beth at his side he'd be equal to any man on earth.

Nelda saw the look that passed between the two and smiled with unusual tenderness. "When's the wedding?"

"Uh, we haven't set a date yet," Beth replied hurriedly. "But we'll let you know as soon as we do."

"We'll have a shower at the office," promised Nelda.

185

"Well, it's time we left you alone." She patted Beth on the cheek and after several more good-byes, left with Dutch.

Kaler got right to the point. "You can't really want to marry me, Beth."

"Of course I can. I do."

"You want to live like this?" He glanced around.

"No, but then we aren't going to live like this. We'll live in a proper house and my folks have several nice old pieces in the attic that will look great once they're refinished and—"

"And you're out of your mind," he interrupted gently. He put his hand flat over her mouth. "Now, just listen a minute and then think through what I'm about to say. Agreed?"

She nodded her head. He removed his hand. "But, Kaler—"

His palm over her mouth, the center moistened by her lips, he said bleakly, "You have to understand, Beth, that every time there's money missing and I'm in the vicinity, I'll be under suspicion. As my wife, you'd be part of that. You'd be part of my past—"

"Mmmmphffft," she said angrily. He relented, but as he took his hand away she grabbed it and held on for dear life. "It's not where you've been that matters, but where you're going."

"I know that, but there are people who look only at the trail behind you. Those are the people who will hurt you, Beth, in a thousand little ways. I don't want you hurt, not at all, not ever."

"It would hurt me not to marry you," she said sadly.

"Oh, God, Beth, I love you so much, but I'm not good enough for you. I want to marry you, but—"

"Of course you're going to marry me. I love you and I want to share this life with you. You're perfectly good for me. So when, do you think?"

"Oh, Beth." He cradled her cheeks in his palms and

186

gazed at her with such open love that her heart skipped erratically. "I'll marry you tonight if you really want me."

She solemnly studied his face, his beautiful face. His eyes were darkly silver, flashing and alive. His very masculine mouth was curved in a tenderly sweet smile. His dark hair fell boyishly over his brow. He looked younger and happier than she'd ever seen him. Stretching out her hand, she gently brushed his hair back.

"I think, you know," she said musingly, "that I've always known you were different. Even way back in school. Anytime the talk was about you, I sat up and listened. Anytime you were around, I stood and stared. Maybe I've always loved you, even all those years ago."

"Hush, don't," he said. He trapped her hand within his and kissed it, front and back. "I don't want to think that you might have loved me then, that I might have escaped all the years of loneliness. I don't want to think of the might-have-beens. I only want to think about the will-bes in store for us."

"And the nows," she added, giving him a kiss.

"And the nows," he agreed, giving her his heart.

LOOK FOR NEXT MONTH'S
CANDLELIGHT ECSTASY ROMANCES®:

CANDLELIGHT Ecstasy Supreme

☐ 37 **ARABIAN NIGHTS,** Heather Graham..................................10214-6-28

☐ 38 **ANOTHER DAY OF LOVING,** Rebecca Nunn......................16789-2-12

☐ 39 **TWO OF A KIND,** Lori Copeland..19082-7-10

☐ 40 **STEAL AWAY,** Candice Adams..17861-4-29

☐ 41 **TOUCHED BY FIRE,** Jo Calloway.......................................19015-0-12

☐ 42 **ASKING FOR TROUBLE,** Donna Kimel Vitek......................10334-7-15

☐ 43 **HARBOR OF DREAMS,** Ginger Chambers............................13446-3-14

☐ 44 **SECRETS AND DESIRES,** Sandi Gelles..............................17675-1-17

$2.50 each

At your local bookstore or use this handy coupon for ordering:

DELL READERS SERVICE—DEPT. B394A
P.O. BOX 1000. PINE BROOK. N.J. 07058

Please send me the above title(s). I am enclosing $_____ (please add 75¢ per copy to cover postage and handling.) Send check or money order—no cash or CODs. Please allow 3-4 weeks for shipment.

Ms./Mrs./Mr._____

Address_____

City/State_____Zip_____

Candlelight
Ecstasy Romances™

$1.95 each

All-new

Candlelight Newsletter

An exceptional, *free* offer awaits readers of Dell's incomparable Candlelight Ecstasy and Supreme Romances.

Subscribe to our all-new CANDLELIGHT NEWSLETTER and you will receive—at absolutely no cost to you—exciting, exclusive information about today's finest romance novels and novelists. You'll be part of a select group to receive sneak previews of upcoming Candlelight Romances, well in advance of publication.

You'll also go behind the scenes to "meet" our Ecstasy and Supreme authors, learning firsthand where they get their ideas and how they made it to the top. News of author appearances and events will be detailed, as well. And contributions from the Candlelight editor will give you the inside scoop on how she makes her decisions about what to publish—and how *you* can try your hand at writing an Ecstasy or Supreme.

You'll find all this and more in Dell's CANDLELIGHT NEWSLETTER. And best of all, *it costs you nothing.* That's right! It's Dell's way of thanking our loyal Candlelight readers and of adding another dimension to your reading enjoyment.

Just fill out the coupon below, return it to us, and look forward to receiving the first of many CANDLELIGHT NEWS-LETTERS—overflowing with the kind of excitement that only enhances our romances!

Candlelight
Ecstasy Romances™

$1.95 each